BETTING GAME

orca sports

BETTING GAME

HEATHER M. O'CONNOR

ORCA BOOK PUBLISHERS

Library and Archives Canada Cataloguing in Publication

O'Connor, Heather, 1960–, author
Betting game / Heather M. O'Connor.
(Orca sports)

Issued in print and electronic formats.
ISBN 978-1-4598-0930-7 (pbk.).—ISBN 978-1-4598-0931-4 (pdf).—
ISBN 978-1-4598-0932-1 (epub)

I. Title. II. Series: Orca sports
PS8629.C624B48 2015   jC813'.6   C2015-901722-X
C2015-901723-8

First published in the United States, 2015
Library of Congress Control Number: 2015935527

Summary: In this high-interest sports novel, a star player on an
elite soccer team is forced to make tough choices when
illegal gambling gets him in way over his head.

*Orca Book Publishers is dedicated to preserving the environment and has printed
this book on Forest Stewardship Council® certified paper.*

Orca Book Publishers gratefully acknowledges the support for its publishing
programs provided by the following agencies: the Government of Canada
through the Canada Book Fund and the Canada Council for the Arts,
and the Province of British Columbia through the BC Arts Council
and the Book Publishing Tax Credit.

Cover photography by Getty Images
Author photo by Jonathan van Bilsen

ORCA BOOK PUBLISHERS
www.orcabook.com

Printed and bound in Canada.

18 17 16 15 • 4 3 2 1

For my children, who taught me to play.
For Mom and Dad, who taught me to read
and made me believe I could do anything.

Chapter One

Ten minutes left in the match and here he comes again. Number 10.

He fakes out our midfield, doing step-overs like a Neymar wannabe. But that won't work on me. I've been shutting him down all night, and it's making him crazy.

It's making me crazy too. Because we always beat Port Peterson. We pay for our wins in blood and bruises, but we always win.

Tonight? I glance at the two guys icing injuries on the bench. We've got the blood and bruises, but we're still chasing our first goal.

Come on!

I ambush number 10 outside the eighteen-yard box and jockey. He touches the ball through, but I get a toe on it. Then he somersaults over my foot.

He could get a gold medal for a dive like that. Or a yellow card.

He rolls around like his leg is broken. Correction: a gold medal *and* an Academy Award.

The ref whistles the play.

"Called that one," I mutter. "Drama queen."

I set up the ball for a free kick. But the ref whistles again and pulls out a yellow. For me!

I roll my eyes. "Seriously, ref?"

Number 10 jumps up and smirks at me.

I clap my hands. "Nice performance, jerkface. Miraculous recovery."

"Forget it, Jack," Alex yells from the net. "Grab a man."

"No problem, bro." I follow number 10.

The free kick is perfect. So is the elbow number 10 lands when we go up to head the ball. I end up flat on my back counting stars. Son of a—

A whistle? Must be the elbow. Good call, ref.

Wait—cheering? They scored on that header?

I sit up, and everything spins. Hands pull me to my feet and steady me until the black fades.

Alex's face swims into view. "You all right, bro?"

"Yeah." Then I see number 10 and lunge. "But I'm going to kill that guy."

I must've hit my head harder than I thought. I can't reach him. Then I figure it out. Alex won't let go of my shirt.

"Don't be stupid, Jack. Just get it back."

But the ball barely clears the center circle when the game ends.

We've lost. To Port fricking Peterson.

Chapter Two

Alex and I leave the training center as the dome goes dark and the last car pulls away. The park is deserted this time of night. The lamp posts that line the path show us the way home.

"We've never lost to Port Peterson before." Alex kicks a stone ahead of him. His voice is quiet. "We were unbeatable in the first half of the season. Top of the table. Now, four games into the spring season, we're 1-1-2. Some captain I am."

He always takes the blame, even at home. Oh, we win as a team. But if we lose, it's all his fault. Part of being a keeper, I guess. Part of being the oldest, even if it's only by ten months. Mom calls him Mr. Responsible.

Now he's wearing the captain's armband. But it's not his fault Jonesy left. "Don't beat yourself up, bro. You heard Coach. It'll take us time to learn to play without Jonesy."

Jonesy left just before spring season started. I heard about it first. I saw him leave Coach's office with this goofy smile on his face. Like the prettiest girl in school had just grabbed him by the ears and kissed him.

"I just got the best news. I can't believe it." He blinked. "I'm going to Liverpool."

"What are you talking about?" I said.

"Liverpool. They want to sign me. To play." He laughed. "In England! I leave in a couple of weeks."

Leaving? It felt like a soccer boot to the gut. Like when Mom and Dad split up.

"But—soccer! And—Liverpool? That's..." That's the Premier League. What every

5

soccer player dreams about. I forced a smile. "That's awesome, man. Congrats."

We lost our captain, our top scorer and our best playmaker, all at once. Alex and I lost our best friend.

Hard to believe the world can turn on its head so fast.

I give Alex's stone a kick. It clangs off a lamp post.

Alex takes everything so seriously. I wish he'd joke around like I do. Or get mad—that burns itself out.

Not Alex. He'd rather chew on it. So I look for a way to fill the silence. "When does our new striker arrive?"

"Late next week. He might make it to a practice. Definitely before our next game. Coach says he's got a great shot."

"See? He can be our secret weapon. When we meet Port Peterson again in June, we'll crush them."

"Deal."

We seal it with a fist bump.

Good thing we're almost home. My eye is throbbing.

"I'm going to pay that guy back for the elbow too. With interest."

Alex looks over. "How is it?"

I touch the swelling with my fingertips and wince. "As big as a tennis ball. Probably twice as pretty."

That makes him smile. "Better ice it again when we get in the door. So you don't scare people."

"Aye, Captain. But I'd rather get an eye patch. Go pirate. You know, in case the crew mutinies. Or the captain abandons ship." I elbow him in the ribs. "'Captain Jack' has a nice ring to it, don't you think?"

He laughs and elbows me back. "In your dreams. I'm not abandoning anyone."

"Arr, matey. Ice it is then."

I throw on a pot of pasta and flip open my laptop while it cooks. "So what do you know about the new guy?"

"Just his name—Gil Joseph."

"That's enough for Google." I type it in pirate-style—holding a bag of frozen peas against my eye. "Check it out. He's got his own YouTube channel."

Alex leans over my shoulder, and I play the first video. It opens with a scrimmage.

"That must be him." I point to a tall blond guy in a blue pinny. "He's quick. Look at him deke their mids."

When he crosses midfield, he chips the defender and races in on a breakaway. He sends the ball into the top corner. Goal!

"Ouch!" says Alex. "The keep didn't have a chance."

The video cuts to shot after shot. Alex and I put on phony Brit accents and pretend to be Premier League commentators.

"Here comes Joseph again. He's charging down the wing."

"He's blazing hot tonight. Just looking for chances. Dangerous, giving him that much space."

"The midfielder tries to keep him outside, but he can't read him at all. A step-over, a lovely little touch and..."

"...he's through! And a nice crisp pass to the middle. Then back to him."

"He left-foots it and..."

The video ends with a beautiful penalty shot. We cheer like it's Man U.

We grab our pasta, and Alex sits down across from me. He's got a big grin on his face. "What a highlight reel!"

"He's a one-man firing squad. Glad he's on our side."

Chapter Three

When I'm done eating, I knock on the laptop. "Fantasy soccer results should be up. Want to see who's doing the dishes this week?"

Alex makes a face. "Sounds more like your fantasy than mine."

"Awww—afraid of getting prune fingers?"

"Shut up, you jerk." He punches me and laughs. "I've seen the scores this week. The only points my guys will get is for field time. I wish Jakobs was playing."

"I can't believe you picked him. I saw him in co-op yesterday. His knee is the size of a soccer ball! He won't be back for months."

"He's a Lancer. Where's your loyalty, bro?"

"I've got plenty of loyalty! But it's not like you picked Benson. He's coming back soon."

He mumbles something.

"Ha! You picked Benson too?" I smack myself in the head. "You can't let personal feelings get in the way of a winning team."

"So you keep telling me. Hand over the laptop. Let's get this over with."

Alex logs on and the stats flash on the screen.

"Big surprise. You beat m—huh." He blinks at the numbers and scrolls down. "How'd you do that? Is this some kind of joke?"

"Do what?" I lean in for a closer look. That can't be right. Can it?

"Let me see that." I log Alex out and try to sign in, but my fingers stumble over the keys.

Finally! *Welcome back, Jack Attack.*

My stomach does a flip. That's my name at the top of the leaderboard. That means... that means...

Alex shouts and laughs and punches me. "Ha! Look at that! You're number one!"

Top team: Jack Attack. I can't believe my eyes.

I knew I had a good week. But this? This is amazing! I jump up and pump my fist.

"Yeah! I am the king!" I put Alex in a headlock. "Say it! Say I am the king."

"You are the—the—" He's laughing so hard he can't get the words out.

"Come on. Say it. I am the fantasy soccer king!"

"You are the...fantasy...soccer king!" he wheezes.

I let him go and check the screen again. "I can't believe this."

"Me neither," says Alex. "You have all the luck!"

"Luck? Do I have to punch you out?"

"No!" He's holding his sides now and gasping for breath. "I—I surrender."

I wag a finger at him. "Luck is for suckers. This takes skill."

He snorts. "Skill. Right!"

"I would be so rich if I could play for money instead of chores."

Alex snorts again.

"Don't believe me? Then tell me. How many weeks did I have dish duty last season?" I cup a hand to my ear. "That's right. Zero!"

"That just means I suck." Alex starts laughing again.

I grin. "You definitely suck. You pick players with broken legs."

Alex is laughing too hard to argue. "Yup."

"But I beat everyone. Thousands of people." I raise my arms like a prizefighter. "I am the fantasy soccer king! And that's why I will be managing Manchester United in ten years, bro. And why you will still be washing my dishes."

We head to bed around ten thirty, but I'm so pumped I can't fall asleep. Mom comes in around eleven and tiptoes in to check on us. Then the phone rings. She hurries to her room to pick it up. I can tell by the edge in her voice that it's Dad.

"Of course they're not up, Rick. Look at the time...We were all out. The boys had a game, and I had to work late...No, I don't know if they won...You should've asked before you bought the tickets. That's a school night."

Tickets? Must be a Lancers game!

"I know. But soccer already takes up a lot of their time. They need to study. Universities look at their grade-eleven marks."

Then she sighs.

"All right. I'll ask them...No, not now. In the morning."

She knows we'll say yes. Before Mom and Dad split up, we had season tickets. Now we only go when Dad feels guilty.

"I wish you'd just pay your child support instead of buying tickets. The boys need... Of course. A client gave them to you."

She sighs again. I know what that means.

"I don't want to get into it, Rick, okay?...
Yeah, I'll tell them."

"Psst, Alex! You awake?" I throw a
balled-up sock across the room, and it
bounces off Alex's head.

"Huh? What?"

"That was Dad. I think he scored
Lancers tickets."

"Mmm..."

I hope it's the Portland game.

Chapter Four

I was right about the tickets. And the team.

I wait for Dad at our usual spot outside the south gate. Fans flow around me, shouting, singing and sounding horns. A familiar whistle cuts through the noise, and I find Dad in the sea of red shirts and waving flags. It takes us a while to shuffle through the crowds at the gate and work our way up the ramps. Enough time for me to tell Dad about our game and explain the shiner.

"Where are the tickets?" I raise my voice over the buzz.

"Same as always," Dad says. "Halfway up. Corner of the eighteen-yard box."

My favorite spot—high enough to see the action, close enough to watch the goals. Right where our season tickets used to be.

The stadium is almost full, and it's still fifteen minutes to kickoff.

"Too bad Alex didn't come," says Dad. "He's going to miss a great game."

"Too much homework."

"How about you?"

"No homework in co-op." I grin.

"Right! You're working with the Lancers. I bet your coach pulled strings for that! What have they got you doing? Taping up ankles?"

"Come on, Dad—I'm seventeen. I can't treat anyone. But I get to watch everything."

"Watch?"

"That's what co-op is for. I've learned so much already. How to treat injuries. How to recover. How to avoid getting reinjured. And I—"

17

"Well, I guess it's a step up from the boot room. Two steps up from carrying towels."

If he only knew. Laying out towels and supplies is mostly what I do in co-op. Plus filing and setting up equipment.

"There's nothing wrong with carrying towels, Dad. Everyone in the academy has chores."

He sniffs. "Like cleaning muddy soccer cleats?"

"You can learn a lot by looking at cleats. That's another thing the physios taught me."

Dad shakes his head. "I still can't believe they make you work for free."

"We play for free. You'd still be paying for soccer if we played rep."

"Oh, that reminds me. Give this to your mom." He hands me a fat envelope with money in it. "Tell her I'm sorry it's late."

"Sure." Talking to him is like kicking a soccer ball against a wall.

I know something that'll grab his attention. The fantasy soccer league standings.

"Well, look at that!" He thumbs through my team. "Good picks! So tell me, who's winning tonight?"

"The Lancers."

"Is that loyalty talking?"

"Nope. They'll cream Portland, 2-0 or 3-0. Safe bet with Kolo out for Portland and Benson coming back for the Lancers."

He looks up from the phone. "Benson's suiting up?"

"Yeah. We saw him today at co-op. He's not starting, but they'll put him in later."

"How do you know that?"

"I told you. I heard them say it."

"Is that right?" Dad's wearing a smug smile. "Good enough for me then."

A few minutes later, he waves to someone in the stands. "Hey, Luka! Luka!"

A young guy in khakis and mirrored shades comes over. Very *GQ*. The kind of guy who gets top marks from girls and their parents.

"Just the man I wanted to see."

"Rick. Good to see you. I thought you'd be here."

There's something European about his voice.

"I have interesting news for you. Sit with us. We have an extra seat."

"Maybe until the game starts. You know me—I like to watch from the rail." He glances over at me. "This must be one of your hotshot soccer players."

Dad sticks out his chest. "That's right. Pride of the Lancers." I get a warm feeling inside.

Luka reaches over to shake my hand. He grips it hard. "So. Are you Jack? Or Alex?"

"Jack. Nice to meet you."

I move over a seat. He edges past Dad and sits between us.

He points a finger at me. "The left back, yes?"

"That's right." Huh. I guess Dad listens more than I thought. "Alex couldn't come. Too much homework."

"But not you?" Luka gives a half smile. "Rick said you were smart."

He did? I lean back in my seat, trying to look cool. "I'm in co-op. With the Lancers physio team."

"Really! You work with the first team?"

"Since February."

"Lucky you!" He leans forward. "Tell me what it's like."

"You sure? No one ever wants to talk ACLs and rehab plans. At least, not for long."

"I do. That's what I want to study— sports medicine or physiotherapy."

I look at Luka again and dial down his age. He can't be much older than I am. And he's actually interested!

"Well, there's way more to it than I realized." I explain how closely the physios and trainers work with the coaching staff to get a player back on the field.

"They're like a team too."

"Exactly!"

"Is it helpful that you play soccer?" he asks.

"Oh, 100 percent. Knowing the game is key. So is knowing the team. But I've been studying all that for years. I keep stats on the players and the teams. I watch the coaches too. You know, when they sub in players and who they play."

"Hmm. Sounds complicated. But it works?"

Dad pipes in. "Does it work? Show him your fantasy standings, Jack."

"Okay. But it's not easy to see on my phone. The screen's bashed up." I'm amazed it still turns on, actually. It's practically an antique.

"Here, use mine." Luka hands me his phone, and I pull up the fantasy league.

I point to my name.

"That's you? You're Jack Attack?"

"The one and only."

"What did I tell you? Smart as they come." Dad reaches over and punches my shoulder. "So, Luka, what's the spread on tonight's game?"

"Lancers by two."

"Good. Put me down for a hundred on the Lancers."

Luka's eyebrows go up. "That's an interesting wager."

"Jack's advice, actually."

A hundred bucks? On my advice? Cool!

Wait, what advice?

"He says Benson's back in form. Tell him, Jack."

"Dad!" I give him a dirty look.

He just holds up his hands. "What? That's what you told me."

"Not so you could spread it around."

Luka sounds confused. "Spread what around, Rick?"

"They're putting Benson in."

Luka's mouth opens, but the loudspeaker drowns him out. The players file out, and the fans rock the stadium.

We rise for the national anthem. The music fills me here like it never does at school. I stand tall and straighten my shoulders.

I'm part of this club. One day it could be me down there. *My* name the crowds shout. *My* face on the Jumbotron.

Stamping feet, whistles and cheers drown out the last notes and shake the stands. I feel it rumble in my feet. On my skin. The wave of sound is so dense, I could crowd-surf on it. This is why Alex fills his fantasy roster with Lancers. Even the broken ones.

Chapter Five

A few minutes into the game, Dad goes for a beer.

Luka leans over. "So. You really think Benson will play?"

"He's dressed, isn't he?"

"He's dressed for every game."

"You watch. He'll sub on in the second half."

He weighs my words with a half smile. "If he plays, he could change the game."

Heather M. O'Connor

He pauses for a moment. "So. How much did you bet on the game?"

"Me? I can't bet."

"Depends on who you know." He looks at me over his shades. "You know me."

I drop my voice. "You'd place a bet for me?"

"Sure. How much?"

"Twenty." I dig out two wrinkled tens, my lunch money for the week. I'll be eating peanut butter sandwiches if I lose.

He makes a face. "Oh, Jack Attack. Nickels and dimes. Fat news like that, I'm betting $1,000."

A thousand? My face burns. Luka must think I'm an idiot.

I pat my pockets for more and hear a crackle of paper. Now that's what I call luck!

He's already on his cell. "Yes, $1,000 on the Lancers by two. Oh, and twenty—"

"Wait!" I check over my shoulder. Dad's nowhere in sight. "Make it fifty."

He nods his approval.

"Make that fifty on—" He stops.

"Hang on," he tells the guy on the phone. He cocks his head. "You have fifty, Jack Attack?"

Have I got fifty? His opinion of me goes up at least three grand when I riffle through the crisp bills in the envelope. "As long as you can change a hundred."

The half smile's back. He puts the phone to his mouth again. "Yes. Fifty on the Lancers."

I stretch out my legs and try to look cool. But it's not easy. I feel like jumping or shouting. Or telling someone!

A few minutes later, his phone rings. He looks at the number. "I have to take this." He gives an apologetic shrug. "I'm sorry. It's business. But I'll be back." He stands up and heads up the stairs.

He passes Dad on his way back. Dad toasts him with his beer, and Luka nods.

"Nice guy, eh?" Dad says.

That's just what I'm starting to think.

My first real bet. It bumps the game up to a whole new level. Like watching a movie on

IMAX instead of a laptop. Or hearing your favorite band live. No wonder people bet on sports.

By the end of the half, I'm sitting on the edge of my seat. Still no score.

What if I'm wrong? I lose fifty bucks. Dad's down a hundred. And Luka—he bet a thousand!

Benson will fix it. He makes everyone better.

Just put him on and it'll be okay.

Put him on soon.

It doesn't seem to bother Dad a bit. He goes for another beer.

It doesn't seem to bother Luka either. A few minutes later, he slides into the seat beside me with pizza slices and pop for both of us. He doesn't ask about Benson. Just, "Pepsi or 7-Up?" Then he asks how I got so good at fantasy soccer.

"Not asking for secrets. Just curious," he says.

"Alex thinks it's just luck, but it's not. I have a system. You know, statistics and probability. I keep track of playing minutes, head-to-head records, player stats. All on spreadsheets. There are too many variables to be right 100 percent of the time, but if you weight them—"

"Enough! I believe you!" Luka laughs and holds up his hands. "I knew you were a smart one. Not everyone bets with their brains. People count on hunches, birthdays, chance. That's fine for lottery tickets. But if I put money on a game, I want more than luck on my side."

"That's what I say. Luck is for losers."

"You know, if you bet real money, you'd be rich." He cocks his head. "I could set you up with an account. You could log in, check the odds, place bets."

"Really?" My mind starts spinning. I could save up for school.

And then I wince. Five bucks here and there, no problem. But online betting? "I don't know. My parents would kill me."

"Who will tell your parents? Not me. Not you."

I wouldn't even tell Alex. He'd flip.

"What's it cost?"

"Nothing if you win."

"It's legal?"

"Not in Canada. But it's on the Internet, so it's all good. It must be okay—your dad has an account."

Luka hands me his phone. "I'll tell you what. Give me your number. I'll set up an account. You want to use it? Great. I'll give you my number too. You want to talk soccer or sports medicine, call me."

He chuckles when he sees my phone. Cracks crisscross the screen. A chunk the size of a nickel is missing.

"Call 9-1-1, Jack Attack. Somebody shot your phone."

"Yeah, it's pretty pathetic." I give an embarrassed laugh. "Here. Let me do it."

The second half of the game is as tense as the first. Where's Benson anyway?

They sub him on at the sixty-minute mark. Finally. Now I can breathe again. "Right on schedule."

Luka's at the rail. Dad flashes him a told-you-so look and gets a big thumbs-up in return.

Three minutes later, we jump to our feet. *Goal!* Benson scores the first point of the game, bending in a free kick that just kisses the crossbar.

The replay on the Jumbotron shows Benson pumping his fists in the air and getting mobbed by half the team.

With four minutes left, he picks up the ball at half. He snakes down the line, dodging two defenders, and sends in a beautiful cross. *Goal!!* The Jumbotron flashes, *He's baaack!*

I look over at Luka. He nods.

We're up 2-0. We've won the game, but have we won the bet? Not if Portland scores again. Fans start leaving, and I crane my head to watch the final minutes. By the end, my throat is raw. What a finish!

I'm up a cool fifty! Luka quietly slips it to me on our way out.

"Thanks, Jack Attack. I'll be in touch."

When I get home, I check my phone. Luka has left me a text.

set u up :) here's the link

username: jackattack

pw: h0tsh0t
meet u for coffee to show u how it works
saturday @ 1:00 good for u?
I text him back.
sure!
And I click on the link.

Chapter Six

I look for Alex the next day after co-op. I find him in the academy classroom.

"So how was the game?"

"Awesome." So was winning fifty bucks. But there's no way he's hearing about that.

"I heard Benson scored both goals."

"Yup. It was magic. Would've told you when I got in, but you were already snoring. Still studying?"

"Nope." He closes his laptop. "I couldn't cram another trig rule in my head if I tried."

He checks his watch. "Anyway, I told Coach I'd show the new guy around before we practice. He should be here soon. Want to come?"

"Sure."

We grab our coats and wait outside the big glass doors of the Lancers Training Center. I can't wait to see the look on Gil's face when he sees it.

Even after three years, I can't believe we belong here. A major-league soccer academy. We're a free kick away from the pros.

We wouldn't be here without Jonesy.

It was the first year of high school, right after our parents split up. New school. New house. New city.

The day we moved in, we heard a knock at the door. And there was Jonesy, with a soccer ball in his hands and a big grin on his face. "You play footie, mates?" He sounded just like Harry Potter.

I elbow Alex. "Remember meeting Jonesy?"

He never gets tired of the story. "Best trick we ever played."

I have to sit up straight and tuck in my chin to get his accent right. "I'm Khalil Jones. I'm with the Lancers Academy."

Alex laughs. "When you handed him a soccer ball and asked for his autograph, he didn't know whether to sign it or punch you in the face."

"And then at the field, whoosh! You stopped his first shot with a perfect layout. His mouth just opened and closed, but nothing came out."

"And you kept stealing the ball from him."

"How was he supposed to know we played rep?"

Another guy might've held it against us. Not Jonesy. He laughed right along with us. Just like that, we were best friends. And the next day, he brought the coach of the Durham Lancers Soccer Academy to our door.

I hope it's that easy with Gil.

"So what do you think he's like?" I ask.

"Gil?" Alex shrugs. "Hard to tell from the video. But we're about to find out." He nods at a guy marching across the parking lot.

I squint. Blond buzz cut, pressed camos, army-green T-shirt. Soccer bag. That's him.

When he gets to us, Alex smiles. "Gil, right?"

"Yeah." He sticks out his chin and tacks on a silent *What are you going to do about it?*

"Thought so. Coach asked us to show you around. I'm Alex, the captain. This is my brother, Jack."

Gil looks from me to Alex. Same black hair. Same chin. Are we...

Alex answers the question before he asks it. "Nope, not twins. Just born the same year."

"Even our mom thinks we look alike. She gives one of us a black eye now and then. Helps her tell us apart." I point at mine. "It was my turn."

He gives me an odd look.

"We saw your YouTube videos," says Alex. "Wicked shot! Where have you played?"

"All over. Europe mostly."

"Wow! What're you doing here?"

"We move a lot."

"Well, I hope you stick around. Let's get started." Alex opens the big glass doors and spreads his arms wide. "This is the Lancers Training Center. Home of the Durham Lancers and the Lancers Academy, one of the top academy programs in North America. We train here, eat here, play here."

He opens the door to the gym and cardio studio. "Weights, bikes, ellipticals. Go in and take a look if you like."

Gil cuts him off. "I've seen gyms before."

"Have you seen therapy rooms before?" I point to ours as we pass and smile innocently. "In case you get busted up."

Alex gives me a dirty look.

I shrug. "Just being helpful."

Alex leads us upstairs. "Here's the dining room. And our classroom, in case you want to do homework."

Next is the viewing theater, my favorite part of the tour. "We use this room a lot," says Alex. "We review our games and watch training films."

Gil's not paying any attention. His too-cool-for-you face is getting annoying.

So I add my own tour talk. "Every Friday is movie night. Blockbuster hits. Popcorn. You can bring a date."

Alex laughs, but Gil's a blank wall.

A challenge. Fair enough.

"He missed Coach's orientation speech. Want me to give him the highlight reel, Alex?"

"Do it!" He grins and sits in the front row. "Wait'll you hear him roll his *r*'s, Gil. He sounds more Scottish than Coach."

Gil leans against the door, his arms crossed.

I mess up my hair and pace around. "Awrrright, lads. I have a few rrrules." I stop in front of Alex and stare him down. He can't keep a straight face. "Keep your eyes and ears on me at all times. I expect your best effort. No lollygagging.

"You must be on time, every time." I tap my watch for emphasis. "The bus will not wait for you. Neither will I."

Gil's next. I wag my finger—classic Coach. "Every one of you thinks you're the next Messi. Even if you are, and I highly doubt it, there's life after soccer. So keep up with your schoolwork. You don't play if you're failing."

No reaction.

Seriously? Someone must've surgically removed his personality.

Alex just rolls with it. He leads him back downstairs. "So here's our locker room, and Coach's office is right around the corner."

"What's wrong with him?" I mouth to Alex. "Is he a robot?"

Alex makes a cutting motion. But I bet he's asking the same questions.

Coach's door is open. He's at his desk, studying a soccer clipboard. He looks up when Alex knocks.

"Coach, this is Gil. We gave him the tour."

"Good lads."

He measures Gil up, then sticks out his hand. "Glad you could join the team, Gil. Here are your uniforms. Practice kit's on top. Red jersey's home, stripes're away. Now get dressed. Let's see what you've got."

Chapter Seven

"Time to meet the team," Alex says. "Good bunch of guys. You'll like them."

I smile, remembering the rush I felt when I walked through this door for the first time. I look at Alex. He remembers it too and grins. He holds the door open to let Gil walk in first, just like Jonesy did for us. But it goes wrong the second he steps through the door.

"What the—" That's all Gil gets out before two half-dressed guys stagger into him. Momentum carries all three of them past the doorway and out of sight. We hear a crash and groans.

"What's going on?" Alex says. We hurry in. Just in time to see the garbage can tip over and water bottles tumble like bowling pins. The team cheers and claps.

The three guys are in a heap. The first one on his feet is Julio.

"Oh, man! Who'd we knock down?" He looks at Gil, flat on his back, and his eyes open wide. "I'm so sorry! We were just messing around. Here, let me help you up."

But he can't. There are water bottles all over the floor, and Danny is sprawled across Gil close enough to give him mouth-to-mouth. Danny kicks at the water bottles, and Gil's arms and legs are going like a flipped-over ladybug's.

I can't help but laugh.

"Nice work, guys," says Alex. "You trying to break him?"

Gil is not laughing. "Get off me, you son of a—" Gil shoves Danny off, swearing under his breath the whole time.

41

Alex and Julio give Danny a hand up. Then they hoist Gil to his feet. He's as red as our jerseys, even his neck.

"Sorry, man!" Now Gil's got hands patting him all over. He slaps them away, huffing like a guard dog choosing who to bite. It's pretty funny.

Until he shoves Danny up against the wall.

Alex grabs his shoulder. "Hey, lighten up. They were just horsing around. They didn't even see you coming."

"Yeah, wasn't D-Man's fault!"

"Get a sense of humor," someone mutters.

No one's laughing now. It's like we chugged a carton of milk and realized it's sour.

"What an initiation," I say. "Seriously, guys. Try a handshake next time."

"Initiation?" says Gil.

Uh-oh. Bad choice of words.

Gil glares at me, then at Alex. "You set me up?"

"No. No! Calm down. Let's try this again." Alex clears his throat dramatically. "Guys, listen up. I'd like you to meet Gil."

"This guy's our new striker?" Danny's still rubbing his neck.

"Not the way I wanted to introduce him. But, yeah."

Gil's watching the team, and I'm watching him. His eyes flick from face to face, then land hard on Alex.

There's going to be trouble.

Chapter Eight

The guys dress and get out, leaving Alex with Gil. What a mess.

The locker room floor is a disaster too. Water bottles. Garbage. Gil's new uniforms.

Alex looks around and sighs. I bet he feels like tossing his captain's armband on the pile.

I start picking up the water bottles. When he tries to help, I shake my head. "I got it. You go ahead. I'll be out to warm you up in a few."

"Thanks, Jack."

Keepers warm up with a partner. I've been filling in since our backup keeper broke his ankle. Coach says I'm his utility player—one size fits all. Alex calls me his backup backup.

Alex is already in the net when I walk on the field. But why is Gil with him? Uh-oh.

Strikers suck at warming up a keep. They think it's a shooting drill.

But it's really a catching drill—the keeper is *supposed* to stop the ball.

Gil lines up balls at the edge of the box. Then he winds up.

Shot after blistering shot. One corner. The other corner. *Bam! Bam! Bam!*

It's like the YouTube video. But it's not cool this time.

Alex dives right and left. He leaps up to the crossbar. There's no time between shots to reset. He can't even get up before another ball whizzes in.

I don't know why Alex doesn't just walk away. I would.

Right after I stuffed a soccer ball down Gil's throat.

The guys stop warming up to watch. They're buzzing. There's no doubt about it. He's good.

And he's still fighting mad.

Probably because Alex is stopping some of his shots. And whenever he does, we cheer.

Coach blows the whistle and calls us in. I wonder how long he's been standing there. I bet he didn't miss much.

The team makes a circle. It opens for Gil but doesn't close around him.

He stands in the gap, eyes front, legs apart and arms crossed. Give him a rifle and a uniform and he'd be G.I. Joe.

"I see you've all met our new striker, Gil Joseph," says Coach.

Gil Joseph, right! His name really is G.I. Joe. I snicker.

"Something you want to add, Jack?"

"Uh, no, Coach. Sorry for interrupting," I mumble.

Alex joins us, and he fills a gap beside Gil.

I meet his eyes across the circle. *What an idiot. You okay?* An imperceptible nod.

G.I. Joe stares at me, and I stare right back. *Listened in, did you? Good.*

"Jack?"

I face forward again. "Yes, Coach."

"Sure you have nothing to say?"

I start to shake my head, then freeze. "I mean—I'm sure, Coach."

"Do a lap and figure it out."

"Yes, sir."

I bend down to tie up my shoelace.

I hear Coach say to Alex, "The goal-keeping coach wants to work with you today. Take a break. He'll be out shortly."

"Okay, Coach." Alex mops his face with his sleeve and limps over to the bench.

As I jog away, Coach says, "The rest of you, grab a partner and loosen up. Properly. I'll be right back."

I knew he was watching. Coach doesn't miss a thing.

Gil is still standing there when I finish my lap. No partner. He either got the cold shoulder or he's waiting for me. I'm stuck with him.

Then Danny breaks away from a group of three and waves me over. I lope past Gil without saying a word. *That'll teach you.*

I turn around to see how G.I. Joe likes the silent treatment.

But I never get the chance. Alex stands up to work with him.

Now I'm mad at both of them.

That's why I share the G.I. Joe joke with Danny. He thinks it's so funny, he spreads it around. By the end of practice, everyone is calling him G.I. Joe or Soldier Boy behind Coach's back.

Everyone but Alex.

Chapter Nine

The locker room is pretty quiet after practice. Alex doesn't say much, even when we're the only two left. But that sure changes on the way home.

"I had to do something. He didn't exactly get the warmest welcome."

"I get that he was mad, Alex. But you take that out on an empty net. Not your keep! Not your captain!"

"You should've left it to me."

"We were teaching him a lesson! You can't treat team like that!"

"Did you treat *him* like team?"

"You're defending him after what he did to you and Danny?"

"No! It's just..." He shakes his head and pauses. When he speaks again, his voice is quieter. "It was my fault things got out of control."

"Your fault? You didn't knock him down. It was an accident!"

"I should've fixed it. I'm the captain."

"Would you skip the 'burden of leadership' crap? He tried to humiliate you. He wanted to show you up! After you showed him around." I throw my hands up in the air. "Argh! What a...a...tool!"

He tries to grab my arm, but I pull away.

"Listen, Jack. It's my job to help him settle in. Like Jonesy did when we joined the team."

"Jonesy would've kicked his ass."

"Yeah? Well, he wouldn't have called him names."

His accusation hangs in the air.

I pinch my lips together.

Alex lets out his breath in a gust. "Think back, Jack. What it was like for us. New town. New team. Remember? And we had each other."

I do remember. I couldn't sleep the night before. But Jonesy made us feel welcome. Like the missing piece that the team needed.

"We've got a game Sunday. Just give him a chance, okay?"

"Fine." It's almost a whisper.

"Thanks, bro."

Chapter Ten

By Saturday I've poked around the account Luka set up for me. It's pretty straight-forward. I just have a couple of questions.

He shows up right on time.

ready to go?

yup

But I'm not ready for the shiny black sports car parked outside.

The tinted window opens silently. "You getting in?" Luka asks. "Or just waiting for a bus?"

"You drive a Corvette?"

"Get in and I'll show you."

The engine rumbles like a World Cup crowd waiting for a penalty shot. He shifts it into gear and we peel out. It's like riding in the Batmobile.

I run my hand along the soft upholstery and lean back in the low-slung seat. Someday I'm getting a car just like this.

He glides into a parking spot at a little café. A bell rings as we go in.

A cute girl in a short black skirt hurries over. She smiles and shows us to a table. Luka says something. She giggles and hurries off.

"What language were you speaking?"

"Russian."

"So you're Russian. I thought I picked up an accent. A little Arnold Schwarzenegger. A little Zlatan."

He purses his lips like I've said something funny. "Not quite. I was born in Ukraine."

The waitress brings our coffee. When I take out my wallet, she puts her hand on mine. "No, no." And she scurries off.

Luka says, "I never pay here. The owner—he's a friend." He sips his coffee. "You look at your account yet?"

I nod.

"Let me show you how it works."

He reaches for my phone and brings up the site.

"Minimum bet is a hundred dollars."

And I tried to bet twenty? What an idiot!

Luka's still explaining. "You win? That's $100 in your account—boom! You lose? Your account goes down by $110. That's $100 plus 10 percent juice."

"Juice?"

"Service charge. But only if you lose."

"Right, juice!" I wave it off. "But how do I get you my bet? I don't have a credit card or anything."

"You don't need one. We settle up once a month. I pay you, or you pay me."

"Okay."

"Remember. You don't bet on who wins or loses. You bet on the point spread."

So as long as my team beats the spread, I win? That means I can bet on the Lancers even if I think they'll lose! Sick!

Luka points at the screen. "Here's where you find the spread. See? Today the Lancers need to win by a goal." He looks at me. "Think they can do it?"

"With Benson back? No problem. The Red Bulls are going down."

"An easy first bet. You're all set."

"That's it? Cool."

He leans back in his chair and crosses his legs. "So tell me. What is it like to play for the academy?"

"Tough work. But awesome!" I start with how hard it is to win a spot, and how you're always working to keep it. And then about getting scouted by pro teams and universities at showcase tournaments. He asks a million questions, including the one everyone asks: Do we hang out with the first team?

"I wish! We aren't even allowed to talk to them, except at club events. I've probably seen more players in my first six weeks of co-op than in two years with the academy."

He's comfortable to talk to. Not awestruck. Just...interested.

Before I know it, my coffee's cold and it's after two. He sees me check my watch.

"Time to go?"

"Game starts at three. I told Alex I'd watch it with him." I waggle my phone and grin. "And if I have time..."

Luka holds up a finger. "And the spread is right."

"...and the spread is right, I might try out my new account."

Luka picks up his keys. "Let's go then. You have work to do."

Before we drive away, Luka reaches behind his seat and pulls out a white box. He tosses it into my lap.

"What's this?" I turn it over and see the Apple logo. Then the model. An Infinity? "No way!"

I turn to Luka for confirmation. He nods, trying not to laugh.

"But...But...they're not even out yet! How did you get it?"

The corner of his mouth twitches. "I know someone."

"Lucky you!"

"Lucky you. It's yours."

Mine? My fingers slide over the picture on the box.

I search his face. "You're kidding me, right?"

"I made a lot of money on the Portland game. This is my way to thank you."

"Oh." My grip on the box tightens. It's a billion times better than my hunk of junk. But I can't take it.

I give it one last look and sigh. "Luka—"

"It's a gift," he repeats.

"But you—"

"I already have one. See?" He pulls an identical phone out of his pocket. "Come on, Jack Attack. It's perfect for you." He smirks and taps the screen. "Completely bulletproof."

I run my fingers over the box again.

I should say, "No, thanks." I should, but I don't.

Chapter Eleven

When I get in the door, I can't decide what to do first. Check out my new phone? Or try out my new account?

Until Alex shouts down, "Jack, is that you?"

I freeze. What was I thinking? Alex knows how broke I am. How will I explain a brand-new iPhone?

His bed creaks, and I hear footsteps.

I've got to hide it. But where? I look around in a panic.

Under the couch.

Alex stops halfway down the stairs. "I thought that was you. You watching the game?"

I glue on a smile. "Wouldn't miss it."

"Great. I'm still working on my trig homework. Call me down before it starts?"

"Sure."

He goes back upstairs.

Yes! That'll give me time to try out my new account.

I punch it in on my old phone. I have to tilt the screen to see around the cracks. This will be so much easier on my new iPhone.

A hundred on the Lancers and...done!

Seconds later, a text from Luka arrives.

good move jack attack ;)

I shout up to Alex five minutes before kickoff. He pounds down the stairs and jumps on the couch.

"Lancers versus Red Bulls. Benson back in action." He sniffs the air and laughs. "Let's barbecue some New York strip loin!"

But it's not as easy as we think.

"What was that?" I shout after another weak cross. "Who were you trying to hit?"

I punch the couch. "They just can't finish today."

If they don't put at least one of those balls in the net, I'm out $110.

"No!" I groan. "Offside again. Be patient."

Alex digs me in the ribs. "Ooh! Getting a little intense tonight. Are some of these guys on your fantasy team?"

My fantasy team? I forgot to check it.

Before I can answer him, the ball comes straight back up the field.

"What a header!" Alex says.

The winger streaks up the line with it. Benson makes a brilliant run forward. He'll be wide open at the top of the box.

My heart's racing. "That's it. Come on!"

"Send it!" says Alex.

The winger times the cross perfectly. Benson catches it on the volley. The ball rockets for the net.

The keeper gets his fingers on it. But it's not enough. The ball sneaks in under the crossbar.

"Goal!" We jump to our feet and do a victory dance. "Yeah!"

But it's a tense fifteen minutes to the end. New York scores a catch-up goal. The ref calls it back. Then, with two minutes to go, the Bulls get a breakaway.

"Don't just stand there!" Alex shouts at the goalkeeper. "Come out."

"Now who's getting intense?"

The keeper darts out. The Red Bulls striker gets off his shot. We lean sideways, willing it wide. And...he misses!

A minute left. Ten seconds.

The ref checks his watch. And—

Time is called!

I'm a little breathless. And a whole lot richer.

The minute Alex goes back to his homework, I check my account. Is it there yet?

Yes! Easiest hundred I ever earned.

Then I reach under the couch for my new iPhone.

I cradle the box in my hands and read about the features. Big screen. Multimedia recording studio. And an unbreakable screen.

Bye-bye, bullet holes. Hello, brand-new world.

I'll figure out what to do about Alex later.

Chapter Twelve

We start fresh with Gil on game day. I think Alex gave the whole team his "Give peace a chance" talk. Gil puts his best foot forward. He doesn't choke or swear at anyone. That's a huge improvement.

It starts off okay. We feed him the ball whenever he calls for it. Which is a lot.

He slams in two goals so quickly that the other team doesn't know what hit them. It's like an instant replay of his YouTube video.

But when he gets the ball, we never see it again. Our mids tuck in for support. The wingers cut into space. He just guns for the net.

The other team catches on pretty fast. They double-team him. Triple-team him. And you need more than fancy footwork and a crack shot to beat a three-on-one.

By mid-game, it's two all.

Coach tells Gil to switch it up. "The rest of you, move it around. Look for opportunities. If Gil's covered, find out who they left open."

It's not as easy as it sounds. The guys up front can't get organized. They make mistakes. So Gil goes back to his first-half game, and so does the other team. Before long, we're down a goal.

Time to change tactics. Gil's not the only guy who's good with his feet.

Next time Alex picks up the ball, I signal to him and catch Danny's eye. Alex slings it my way, and I drive up the field with Danny beside me for the give-and-go. We catch their mids flat-footed. They race to shut us down.

Gil shouts, "Square!" and someone peels off to cover him. That's when I see Julio, all alone on the right. I send over a long ball. He brings it down and zigzags in. Danny, Gil and I sprint for the net, and Julio winds up for the cross. The ball's sailing wide of the far post until Danny flicks it in with his head.

Goal!

Gil glares at Julio, Danny and me coming down the field. You'd think we scored on Alex instead of tying up the game.

An hour after I go to bed, I'm still fuming.

We'll never make the playoffs by putting up a point a game. And we should've won.

I pound my pillow. Stupid Gil.

Alex mumbles in his sleep.

Well, bro, I gave peace a chance. Time to try something else.

But what?

I lie in bed, staring at the ceiling.

Should I push up more often? It worked today.

Could I play box-to-box for ninety minutes? I'd need to crank up my speed and stamina. But that's doable.

I change my alarm clock and smile. Gonna build me some bionic legs.

Starting tomorrow.

Chapter Thirteen

The sky's turning pink as I head into the park. How am I going to do this? A longer route to the training center. Check. Rev up my pace. Check. Add some speed bursts and hills. Fold in the outdoor fitness trail. Check and check. Just made my daily run three times longer and three times harder.

The sun rises as I climb the last hill. I burn it up on the downhill, right to the front door of the Lancers Center.

I could work out like this every morning. It's only April, nearly three months to playoffs.

I'm at co-op before eight, pulling charts and setting up for the players we'll see. I run my ideas by the physio.

Kim purses her lips. "Don't overtrain. You already practice four times a week. Plus your runs and gym time."

"I'm just adding intensity. You know—to bump my performance."

"Feeling a little flat, are you?" She nods slowly. "Okay. No one's coming in for bit. Check in with your trainer. He can ramp up your strength and conditioning program, maybe suggest some new drills."

I shoot her a big smile. "Thanks!"

The trainer gives me the same warning about overtraining. But he promises me new drills and extra time.

"We'll start today. See me after co-op."

Then he makes a great suggestion. "Wouldn't hurt to train your brain too. Coach would probably let you watch game videos in the viewing theater."

"Really?"

"Sure. Study the pros too. You're a Man United fan. Look at Giggs in his prime. Coach could rhyme off a dozen more."

Everything's falling into place.

There's a player on the treatment table when I get back to co-op.

Kim comes over for an ice pack.

"What happened?" I ask. "You get so bored you went out and tripped someone?"

"Wise guy." She grins at me. "He did this on his own. Pulled a hammy in practice."

"Ouch."

"Nothing too serious. Out for a week, maybe two. The TFC game, for sure. Maybe Montreal and DC too. After that, depends how he responds." She can't resist adding, "That's what comes of overtraining, Jack. So watch it."

"Don't worry. Getting injured isn't in my game plan. So how do we treat a pulled hammy?"

I hit the pitch earlier than usual that afternoon to try out my new drills.

Coach is already there. He gives me the okay for the viewing theater. "Whenever it's empty, lad." He cocks his head. "Why the sudden interest?"

"Looking for answers, I guess."

He raises his eyebrows. "To what question?"

"Why we're so...lost."

Coach nods slowly. He hands me a stack of cones, and we lay them out.

How can I explain it?

"I see it clear as day from defense, Coach. Who's open. Who's not. Where we could be two or three passes later."

He stops and eyes me curiously. "Do you now? Like a chess game."

"But we lose shape once the ball leaves our end. We fall apart."

He takes the extra cones. "So what's your plan?"

"I don't know. Work harder. Watch harder." I give Coach a crooked grin. "Gotta start somewhere."

I set up the hurdles and start my first drill. Coach's eyes never leave me.

Like I'm the chess move he's trying to figure out.

In practice, Coach focuses on our passing and playmaking. So do I.

I study each player, breaking down his skills. What he's good at, what needs work. Who he connects with. I chuckle to myself. It's like choosing fantasy-soccer picks.

I watch Soldier Boy too. Turns out he can pass. Until someone makes a mistake. He's too slow, or too sloppy. He doesn't find the net or run into the right space. Or give the ball back fast enough.

It's like Gil's got money riding on every pass. Each bad ball tips the odds until— *bam!*—the guy's cut from his team.

When I figure it out, I'm twice as mad. Does he think he's perfect? That we're his ten-man defense? That we're screwing up his game?

He can't trust us? Then—*bam!*—he's cut from my team.

Coach splits us up for scrimmage.

It's Gil against Alex and me. We'll teach him what a real defense is like. And he better learn quick if we're going to finish this season on top.

Right off the hop, Gil's got the ball. A little touch right, then left, and he's through the mid. He's coming in hard. Here's where he should be setting it up. But he doesn't.

Coach yells, "Pass it around, Gil. You're not Ronaldo."

I call in a second defender, then a third. We slow him down and cut his options. He tries his fancy footwork, but I'm not watching his feet. One good tackle later, and the ball pops out.

I get there first and wait, out of reach, with one foot on the ball. I laugh—I can't help it. Gil looks mad enough to kill his mother.

When he comes in for the challenge, I nutmeg him and go around. He grabs my jersey, but he's too late. The ball's on its way to Danny.

I call over my shoulder, "Even Ronaldo gets beat."

"Yeah, get in the game, Soldier Boy," says Danny.

Next time he comes down the field, Gil throws an elbow. Same eye. Tell me that's an accident.

But it doesn't do him any good.

He uses his wingers too little and too late. They're so surprised to get the ball that we crunch them anyway. Every time Gil goes it alone, I jump on him. We don't shut him down every time, but when he shoves past us, he's still got Alex. And Alex is good.

It feels like hours before Coach lets us go. But I leave the field grinning. I'm under Gil's skin, and it's worth every drop of sweat.

"Learn anything, G.I. Joe?" says Danny. "Because we sure schooled you!"

He can't ignore the snickers. But I don't think he learned a thing.

Chapter Fourteen

Alex and I are the last ones to the dining room.

"You made awesome saves today, Alex!"

"Thanks, bro." He grabs two trays and hands one to me.

"You were a brick wall!" I hold up my tray like a shield. "Every time Gil fired a shot—*ping!* Denied!"

Alex looks away. "So. What's on the menu today?"

He's awfully quiet. I bump his shoulder. "You okay?"

"Sure. Just hungry." He loads up a plate with pasta, then just stands there.

"Coming?" I say.

Alex looks from the team table to Gil. He's sitting by himself, with his back turned.

What's the matter, Soldier Boy? Too good to sit with the team?

Alex frowns a little. "We can't let him sit alone."

"I can."

I watch him walk over to Gil. He gestures at the team table and says something. Gil shakes his head, so Alex shrugs and joins him. Then he looks back at me. "Come on!" he mouths.

Nope. He's backing the wrong team.

I head the other way and grab a spot between Danny and Julio. Danny jerks a thumb in Gil's direction. "You sure yanked his chain in practice. Think it'll teach him to pass?"

"I hope so," Julio says. "I hardly touched the ball today. Next scrimmage, I want to play with you."

Everyone grumbles about Gil. I twirl spaghetti on my fork and listen.

They leave one by one until it's just Danny, Julio and me at the table. I lean in on my elbows and drop my voice.

"Listen, I want to try something. Gil won't play our game, right? So let's play it without him. Like yesterday."

Julio looks puzzled.

Danny's intrigued. "You'll set us up?"

"Yeah. Attack from defense. We're strong enough."

"It's a lot more running," says Julio.

"Only for Jack." Danny grins and punches me.

"Already on it. My trainer ordered me bionic legs."

"See? He's got it covered."

"And I'm going to watch old Premier League games. Giggsy played like this."

Danny raises his hand. "Dibs on Beckham."

I give him a shove. "In your dreams."

Julio's still not convinced. "Did you talk to Coach?"

"Sort of."

Danny snorts.

"Look. We're at the top of the table, and I want to keep us there. Just be ready, okay?"

"I'm in." Danny puts his fist on the table.

Julio adds his fist to the stack. "Me too."

I make it three.

Alex doesn't say much on the way home. Probably still mad at G.I. Joe. He's doing his Captain America best to make him part of the team, and Gil won't pass to us—or even sit with us.

He starts his homework as soon as we get in.

I have my own homework. The TFC game. After staring at the screen for fifteen minutes, I'm no closer to a decision than when I logged on. I'm ready to call it a night when Luka calls.

"Putting anything on the game Friday?" he asks.

"You know what? I'm not. It's too close to call."

"Even with your system?"

"My system's telling me not to bet. If it was a home game, maybe. But not in Toronto. Reds fans are like a twelfth man."

Luka chuckles.

"Plus we're down a defender. He pulled a hammy this morning. They won't play him Friday. Maybe longer."

"Really? That's good to know. Thanks for the advice, Jack Attack."

Now, time for bed. If I want bionic legs, I need the sleep.

Five days of morning runs and extra workouts start to take their toll. My legs are so limp by Friday, the only thing holding them up is my shin pads.

"Doing anything this weekend?" Danny asks after practice.

"Going home, watching the Lancers game and sleeping until Sunday."

"Bionic legs not in yet?"

"Not yet. Bad luck for Alex. He's going to have to carry me home tonight."

I check my watch. "Hey, Alex. Ready to leave? Don't want to miss the big kickoff."

Alex smacks himself in the head. "Oh! I totally forgot to tell you. I made plans for tonight."

"What beats a Lancers game?" Especially when it's TFC. We always watch Toronto games.

"I'm going paintballing."

"Paintballing. Really?" Why won't he look at me? What's going on?

"Yeah, with Gil. It'll be fun. Want to come?"

Gil? He wants me to go paintballing with G.I. Joe? He's pleading for a yes.

I glare at Gil. "Not even if they were real bullets."

A few of the guys laugh. Alex's mouth drops open.

I don't care. I grab my bag and shoulder past.

I avoid Alex all weekend. I'm still ticked on Sunday, on the way to our game.

"So, uh, how was the Lancers game?" he asks as we cut across the park.

"Skipped it. I watched old Man U games instead."

"Oh." He tries again. "You should've come paintballing. It was fun."

I just keep walking.

"You'd like Gil."

Give it up. I stare straight ahead and walk a little faster.

"He's not a bad guy. Once you get to know him."

"Except he's practically nonverbal," I mutter.

Alex scrunches up his face. "Gil's kinda like a ketchup bottle. Takes him a minute to get started."

Alex's ketchup, on the other hand, seems to be flowing just fine. And if he doesn't put a lid on it, I'm going to blow.

"He's traveled all over, you know. He's seen all the big European teams play. Man U. Barcelona. Bayern Munich."

Shut up!

But he doesn't.

"When his dad was posted in England, they had season tickets to Chelsea. He even played for some of the Premier League academies."

I stop in the middle of the path and jam my hands on my hips. "Well, that explains everything."

"Huh?"

"Why he thinks the Lancers Center is a dump. Why he's too good to play with us or even talk to us. He'd rather play in the Premier League."

Alex's eyebrows go way up, then crash.

"Forget it," he mutters. "Just forget it." He doesn't say another word all the way to the game.

We win.

It's no thanks to me or my grand plan. My legs are so tired that I can barely hold my own position.

G.I. Joe scores our only goal, which makes me mad enough to spit ketchup. Instead, I bottle it up and walk home alone.

Luka calls that night. "Jack Attack. You were right about the TFC game."

"I didn't watch it."

"I did. No score. And it was boring. You didn't miss anything."

"Glad I didn't bet then."

"Me too." He pauses. "For a guy who didn't lose a bet, you sound...not so happy. Did you lose your game?"

"No, I just didn't play my best game."

"Maybe the DC game will be better. Someone gave me tickets. Want to go?"

"Sure. I would, actually. As long as you don't mind picking me up from my game."

"No problem," he says. "So. Will your defender be back for the DC game, or is he still limping in to see you every day?"

"He's still out. But the Lancers won't need him this week anyway."

"No?"

"They'll kill Montreal, even with that spread. And we're going to own DC United. Their U23s are at a National Team camp. I put a hundred dollars on both games."

"I saw that. And Benson. He's still okay?"

"Better than ever."

"Sounds like it will be a good game then. See you Sunday."

"Thanks, Luka. You really know how to cheer a guy up."

Chapter Fifteen

By game day, my bionic legs are finally kicking in. I can't wait to try them out.

We give G.I. Joe the first half. He plays his usual game, so I signal Danny and Julio. Next time I get the ball, I push up. Danny's on my left, and Julio's up the line. We play keep-away with their mids, nice and slow to give us time to settle. Pass and move. Back and forth. Up the line. Back to me. Nice, crisp triangles that wear them out.

Gil's confused. The other team's frustrated. When their mids get tired of chasing the ball, they creep forward, leaving a big fat hole.

That's when Danny makes a quick break. I give him a through ball that puts him at the edge of the area. He carries it into the box and finds Julio, angling for the far post for the tap-in. Goal!

We fool them again on another play in the second half. The game ends 2–nil. Two for us, nothing for Gil.

We carry the postgame celebration into the dining room. G.I. Joe and Alex are nowhere in sight.

Time to play a trick on Danny. He's such a tech geek. He'll never believe my new iPhone.

The guitar riff from "Dangerous Game" comes from my pocket. Perfect timing.

"Cool ringtone," says Danny as we head for the team table. "I love Calamity Crossing. Did you hear they're coming to town in a few weeks?"

"I heard. Did you get tickets?"

"I wish!"

"Me too. They sold out in the first few hours."

I pull out my phone. It's a text from Luka.

game over?

yup

u win?

yup!

:) cu in 15

k

Danny cocks his head. "New phone?"

I smile to myself. That didn't take long.

"About time! What'd you get?"

I hand it over and watch his eyes pop.

"No way! Hey, look! Jack's got the new iPhone." He holds it up for the whole table to see. "Where'd you get it?"

"From a friend."

"Nice friend!"

"Hey, what's it got?" someone asks.

Danny tells them. "First off, it's immortal. You can't smash it, scratch it or drown it. Jack couldn't kill this thing if he dropkicked it into four lanes of traffic. It's got a live-stream broadcast studio, instant upload, PhoneList."

They pass the phone around.

"What is it—a prototype?"

"He just gave it to you? They're, like, a thousand bucks."

"Yeah, and Danny says you can't even get them yet."

I bet Luka gets this reaction whenever he takes his Stingray for a spin. I just sit back and enjoy it.

Until Alex sits down across from me.

He looks at the phone. At me. The question hangs there awhile.

"Where'd you get it?"

"A friend."

He waits. I shovel food into my mouth and rehearse my answer.

"His name's Luka. I met him at a Lancers game."

I keep eating, eyes on my plate. He had to find out sooner or later.

"Why would he give you a brand-new iPhone?"

"I don't know." I unscrew my Gatorade and take a sip. "His family must be rich—he drives a Corvette. That reminds me." I look up at the clock. "He's giving me a lift home. See you later, Alex."

That's all you're getting, bro.

The guys are still huddled around my phone.

"Gotta run, guys. Toss me my phone." I catch it one-handed.

As I head down the stairs, I spot G.I. Joe leaving Coach's office. Coach must've burned his ears. About time.

I match my pace to his. We march through the front doors like we're on parade. The only sound is the squeak of our running shoes.

Luka pulls up, and Gil's eyes follow the sleek black sports car. When I get in, his mouth drops open.

Ha! Soldier Boy's not as stone-faced as I thought.

Luka and I have a long conversation about soccer injuries on the way to the DC game.

He asks really good questions. How long do injuries usually sideline a player? The pulled hammy, for example. How do we know a player's ready to come back? Who makes those decisions? I can tell he's impressed by how much I know.

We talk right through the game. The Lancers beat the spread, just like I said.

"Another win, Jack Attack," Luka says on the way to the car.

"Yup." I kick an imaginary free kick. "Counting tonight, I'm five for five."

Before we pull away, Luka counts out what he owes me.

"Not bad for your first month, Jack Attack." The corner of his mouth turns up. "Not bad at all."

I pull out the cash when I get home and start spending it in my head. This is too cool!

Then I count the games in the Lancers schedule. Even at a hundred dollars a pop, I could make four grand by the end of the season. Luka's right. Not bad at all.

Chapter Sixteen

All the extra hours on the field and in the gym are paying off. I've got jets on my feet. New moves in my playbook. I've never been fitter. And it shows.

I got the ball rolling with Danny and Julio. Now it's time to bring in the rest of the team. I work with new partners at every practice, pumping up their confidence, figuring out how to get them the ball, talking it over after.

It comes together, bit by bit. Before long, we kick serious butt. We start to hold our shape again and score more goals. It's a team effort.

Well, mostly. No point getting Gil involved. He's not a team player, on the field or off. He hardly says a word to anyone but Alex. Even then, Alex does most of the talking.

Alex is G.I. Joe's new BFF. They eat together, hang out together, sit on the bus together.

All the stuff my brother used to do with me.

I've got more important things to do. I watch game films in my spare time for fresh ideas. Our games and first-team games, as well as the best teams in history. Man U with van der Sar between the pipes. Barca. Real Madrid. Bayern Munich.

I study how soccer's best playmakers get the job done. I take apart their attacks, replaying them again and again. I want to think like Fàbregas. Challenge like Yaya

Touré. Sometimes Coach watches with me. I ask him questions, and he always asks a few of his own. He adds names to my watch list too—Xavi, Iniesta and Pirlo.

But today he has more on his mind than game films. He pulls up a chair and sits across from me.

"You said you were looking for answers last month. Well, lad, my eye's been on you ever since. I've never seen you put forth so much effort. You're not just playing faster. You're playing smarter."

"Thanks, Coach. I'm doing my best." I smile to myself. He never misses a thing.

"It shows. Your initiative on the attack is changing how we play. I like it. I'd like to bump you up to mid sometimes. Give you better opportunities to score. What do you think?"

"That would be great!" I'd call the shots, right in the heart of the game.

He purses his lips for a moment. "You know, I always thought you held back a wee bit with Jonesy. But you've really stepped it up since he left. You're bringing the other lads along for the ride too. That kind of team leadership will get us to the playoffs. It might get you to first team someday. Or to coach."

I should be proud, but I feel a little guilty. I didn't come up with this plan because Jonesy left. Not exactly.

"However..."

Uh-oh.

"Whatever's between you and Gil"—Coach leans forward—"work it out. We're fighting two other teams for those playoff spots. Every win counts. Maybe every goal." He wags his finger at me. "And every player too. So keep your personal issues off the pitch and off the scoreboard."

I'll do my best, but Coach doesn't understand how personal it is. I can't leave Gil at the field. Alex brings him home.

Not physically. Not yet anyway. But he talks about him. Asks me to hang out with them. Tells me I should be *nicer*.

Nicer. Like he's my mother. Like *I'm* the bad guy.

Playing the good captain makes him suck as a brother. So yeah. It's personal.

Good thing my workouts keep me so busy. Good thing I met Luka.

Chapter Seventeen

Luka says I have the longest winning streak he's seen in months—seven straight games.

"Impressive, Jack Attack. Must be your system."

So then what do I do? Something stupid.

I slap down $250 on the next game instead of my usual $100. A one-point spread against Vancouver seemed like such a smart idea at the time.

Not anymore. Not when the full-time score is 0–0.

Stupid Lancers. You couldn't score one goal? I slam the laptop closed and kick the wall. I should kick myself instead.

Mom calls up. "Everything okay?"

"Yeah. Just, uh, dropped something."

Yeah—$275, with the juice. That's $75 more than I won this month.

Not good! I check my wallet, but all I can scrape together is twenty bucks. The $350 I won in April is long gone. How will I pay Luka next week? What if I can't?

The only game left this month is Seattle, and the spread sucks. I'm not sure it's worth the gamble.

Luka's not sure either. When we go for coffee the next day, he says, "So. You think the Lancers will take Seattle?"

I breathe in the steam that rises from my coffee before answering. "Well, the Lancers have won the last four matchups. Our treatment room's pretty empty, so everyone's healthy..."

"But..."

"But the Sounders are top of the table."

"They've dropped two of their last three games."

"That's true."

He leans forward. "So you think the Lancers will beat them."

"We have before. I just don't think we will this time."

"Then you'll take the Sounders?"

I shake my head slowly. "Nope. I already made one dumb choice this month. Look where it got me. So unless you want to depend on luck..."

"Luck? That's the best you can do?" One of Luka's eyebrows goes up. "I'll get a lottery ticket."

We sip our coffee in silence. I rub a smudge off my phone with one thumb and flick a look at Luka. I'm going to have to tell him.

"So, Luka, this month. Between Vancouver and Seattle. Well, I'm a little short."

He puts down his cup. "It happens."

"It does?"

"Sure."

I wish I could see his eyes through his shades. "What happens...exactly, if I can't pay you Monday?"

He shrugs. "You pay interest. Ten percent. Like juice."

That's a relief.

He must've heard me thinking. "Ten percent. Daily. You don't want to get behind. It adds up. Very fast."

"Don't worry. It's just $75. I'll have it by Thursday. I've got a good feeling about the LA game. I bet $200."

Luka's half smile twitches. "You won't bet against the Sounders, but you'll bet against LA Galaxy? Your system tells you this?"

"That's right." I lean back and cross my arms.

"Even though LA just needs to win by one goal."

"That's why I'm betting." I pull in my chair and sit up straight. "See, LA is primed for a loss. The Lancers are building, now that Benson's back. Player for player, we can beat them! And when we win—"

"If. If they win."

"—it'll more than cover the seventy-five dollars."

"If you say so, Jack Attack."

Luka scores tickets. For once, I wish he hadn't. It's a disaster. LA scores four minutes in. Again six minutes later.

The Lancers fall apart.

The fourth goal rolls in at the thirty-two-minute mark.

"What are you doing out there?" I shout.

Luka throws up his hands. "It's over. Want to grab a coffee?"

"Yeah. I can't watch any more of this."

The pretty waitress serves us, but even her shy smile can't cheer me up. I lost. Again! Now I'm down almost $300. My mood's as black as the coffee.

"Misery loves company, Luka. How much did you bet?"

"Me?" He looks surprised. "Nothing."

Figures. At least he doesn't say, "I told you so."

"Don't worry, Jack Attack. You'll win it back. Your system, remember?"

But I am worried. This *was* my system.

As soon as I get home, I study the games for June. The first bet is a no-brainer—$300 to square things with Luka. Then I look at the rest.

It cheers me right up. They're giving away money on all three Lancers games—the spreads are amazing. I bet $500 on each of them. It's going to be a good month. By the end of June, I'll win back five times what I lost.

Chapter Eighteen

June is a good month for the team too. The move to midfield gives us just the boost we need. It's never for a full game, and Coach still needs me to hustle back on defense. But we're scoring more. We're connecting.

It's not perfect. But sometimes? Sometimes it feels like Jonesy's back.

The biggest surprise is Gil. Every now and then someone passes to him—a last resort, usually—and Gil delivers. It makes me wish he wasn't such a jerk.

Especially today. I play my best game of the season. I set up Julio and Gil, and I score the third goal myself. It's a beauty. It rockets into the top corner from twenty-five yards out.

Gil never gets involved in the rowdy goal celebrations. Nothing special about that. But as we cross the center line, he says, "Good game." He doesn't look at me. Just lines up for the kickoff like nothing happened. But I know what I heard.

It's a first. I'm almost too surprised to answer. "Thanks!" And then I add, "You too."

I jog back to my position.

"So what did Soldier Boy want, applause or a salute?" Danny says it extra loud, for Gil's benefit.

My hands curl into fists. "Shut up, Danny." I stare after Gil, hoping he didn't hear. But I'm pretty sure he did.

I don't sound like that, do I?

After the game, Coach lays it out.

"All right. I like what I'm seeing. Two games left, lads. Greenwood this week.

Port Peterson next week. Both top teams. Both fighting for the same two playoff spots.

"We need to win them both." He looks at each of us in turn and shakes his finger. "It won't be easy. We need to be fit, fast and fresh."

Danny puts up his hand. "Does that mean no all-night parties, Coach?"

Coach just gives him a look.

I elbow Danny. "Didn't you hear? Coach is doing bed checks for the next two weeks. Better get your mommy to tuck you in by seven o'clock."

Everyone laughs, even Coach. But when the laughter dies down, he says, "Joke all you want. But our club hosts the playoffs this year. Think about that for a moment. Nothing could be sweeter than winning at home. Nothing could be worse than watching from the stands. So practice hard and play together. All of you. For team and for pride. You do that, and we might need to clear a spot in our trophy case for a pretty gold cup."

Chapter Nineteen

With two games left, Coach works us pretty hard. But we work ourselves hard too.

The Friday before our Greenwood game is hot and humid. By the time we're through, my muscles feel like toasted marshmallows. Luka texts me when I'm just about to ooze home.

want a ride?

yes!!! sooo tired

"Thanks, Luka!" I close the door and sink into the passenger seat. "Ahhh. Air-conditioning!"

"So, Jack Attack. Big weekend?"

"Nope. Just my game Sunday."

"You're not going to the Calamity Crossing concert tomorrow?"

"Nope."

"I thought you were their biggest fan." He gestures in my direction. "The T-shirt, the ringtone, the tunes..."

I scrunch up my face. "Everything but the tickets."

"But I heard it's the best concert of the year."

"Then you heard how fast it sold out."

"So. I didn't get tickets either." He looks over his shades at me. "But I got something better."

"Better?" I sit up straight. "What's better than tickets?"

"Backstage passes."

"To Calamity Crossing?" My voice comes out in a squeak.

"No, Justin Bieber. Want to go?"

"Do I—" I fall back in my seat. Backstage. With Calamity Crossing. No one will ever believe this.

Then I remember the Greenwood game. And my bank-account balance.

"I can't afford that." I look at my hands and swallow. "I mean, I'd love to, but I'm broke. I'll be okay by the end of the month, and I've got $500 on tomorrow's game, but—"

"Did I ask for money? No. It's a gift." He slants a look at me. "And don't worry about how much you owe. We'll work something out."

Work something out? I squirm in my seat. What does that mean?

"Anyway, I didn't pay for the passes."

"Then how..." It comes to me. "You know somebody."

He points his finger pistol at me and gives his half grin. "Exactly. So we're on?"

I bite my lip. "Don't laugh, but I can't stay out too late. I have a big game the next day."

He doesn't laugh, but his grin twitches. "No problem. I'll drive."

"Then count me in. Thanks, Luka!"

I come into the house ready to burst. I'm going to meet Calamity Crossing! Wait until Danny hears. I'll have to text him.

Alex is at the kitchen table. He looks up as I come in. Like Mom when she wants to talk about something but doesn't know how to start.

"Hey." I give him a wary look and brace myself for questions.

"Dad called," he says.

Sounds safe. No questions yet.

"He got us Lancers tickets for tomorrow night."

"Tomorrow?" I shake my head. "Sorry. Can't go."

He looks relieved and disappointed at the same time. "I didn't know you had plans."

"I'm going to Calamity Crossing."

He gives me a hard look. "How'd you get tickets?"

I shrug. "Luka got backstage passes."

"Luka." And the question marks are back. Before I can escape, he says, "You see a lot of Luka."

"So what?"

"He keeps giving you stuff. A fancy new phone. Lancer tickets. Now backstage passes. Why? Who is this guy?"

Too many good questions. Too many bad answers. Nothing I can tell Captain America.

I force a casual answer. "Just a guy. My friend."

Alex shakes his head. "No one throws around money like that."

I go over to the fridge and look inside. "I told you. He's got rich parents."

"I know. And a hot car. And he drives you around like a chauffeur."

I pour a glass of milk and grab an apple. "I'd offer you a ride, but it's a two-seater."

"I'm not asking for a ride!" Alex slams his hands on the table. He tries again, searching for his normal voice. "What I'm saying is...I've never met him. No one's met him."

"Dad has." Uh-oh. That was stupid.

He looks straight at me. "What's going on, Jack?"

He has the nerve to ask what's going on? Seriously?

"I'll tell you." I count off the reasons on my fingers, one at a time. "One. I don't like your new BFF. Two. You're jealous. Three. None of your business. Get over it."

"This is all *my* fault?"

I hear Mom's key in the front door. No way am I playing tag-team Twenty Questions. I leave my snack on the counter and take the stairs two at a time.

Alex comes up a little later. He knocks on our bedroom door. The lights are off, and I'm pretending to sleep. He comes in anyway. "Sorry, bro," he says quietly. "I'm just worried about you."

I lie very still. Eventually, Alex gets up and goes downstairs again.

Why did I tell him Dad knows Luka? Why?

I take off early the next morning, leaving a note for Mom.

Working today. At a concert tonight. Back late.

I'll kill the day at the training center. Someone always needs a hand. I'll duck back home to change and shower once Alex leaves for the game.

Anything to avoid another conversation with Sherlock Holmes.

I cut straight across the park at a jog. Why did I even open my mouth? What if

Alex grills Dad at the game? Argh! I'm so stupid!

Don't think. Just run.

A runner zips by, and I match his pace.

At least Alex won't meet Luka. He'll be at the concert with me.

But Dad could still tell him Luka's a bookie.

If Alex finds out, I'm dead. He'll tell Mom. Mom will blame Dad.

They'll find out I'm gambling. Then I'll really be in trouble.

I speed up and start the circuit.

But how would they find out? Luka won't tell them. I sure won't. Anyway, I'm winning more than I'm losing. I'll just say Luka's my friend. He is, isn't he?

Maybe Alex will forget about it...

Yeah. And maybe Manchester United will move to Canada.

I pound up the last long hill to the training center. It's all downhill from here.

Chapter Twenty

When Luka picks me up, I'm wearing my favorite Calamity Crossing T-shirt.

We park a few blocks away and go in through an alley. "Got something against lineups?" I ask.

Luka gives his half grin. "Backstage passes. Backstage door."

A guy who could beat up the Incredible Hulk opens the door. His face lights up, and he says something in another language.

Luka laughs, answers him and points at me. The guard opens the door and waves us in.

It's louder than a Lancers game backstage. We dodge roadies carrying equipment and rolling out cables. We squeeze into a quiet spot in the wings.

Before long, the houselights dim. The stage lights come up. The cheers and whistles and stamping from the audience get so loud, we don't even try to talk.

Luka tugs my sleeve. Walking by, close enough to touch, is Calamity Crossing. I fumble for my phone. I'm too late to get their faces. But I turn around and take a selfie with the band walking onstage in the background. Proof I was here.

They play all their best songs. By the end, my eardrums are fried and my throat is raw. "Luka, that was awesome!"

"Time to meet the band."

I can hardly breathe. We walk down the hall and stop at the doorway to a dingy room. Inside, the band and the crew are laughing and cracking open beers.

Luka catches his buddy's eye. He bends down and says something to the guys in the band. They nod, and he waves us over.

I'm going to party with Calamity Crossing. But it's not the thrill I expected.

One after another, the guys in the band sign my T-shirt with a permanent marker. But they don't even look at me. The guard asks for my phone. Without even interrupting their conversation, they strike a well-rehearsed pose. Luka's friend snaps the shot, hands back my phone and leads me away.

Luka is already playing poker. Everyone's having a good time.

Everyone but me. I lean against the wall, trying to look like I belong. But I feel like a kid at a grown-ups' party. A kid with a game to play tomorrow.

The air gets thick with smoke, and my eyes are burning. The cooler of beer empties. After an hour or so, the poker players groan and toss in the cards.

Finally. Now we can get out of here.

Luka gathers up his winnings and strolls over with a beer. "Having fun?"

"I've got to go, Luka. My game."

"Oh." He looks at the beer in his hand. "Take a cab."

"You're staying? But—"

"They invited me to their hotel. Better booze. Better company. You know what I mean?" He drifts back across the room.

I check the time—it's after midnight! I shove my phone into my pocket and glare at Luka's back. He could've told me. Hours ago.

I search for an exit, swearing under my breath. When I finally hit the street, it's raining. The shivery, shoe-soaking, all-night-long kind of rain. Perfect.

The buses better still be running. I check my wallet. Empty. I pat my pockets. No change.

"I can't fricking believe this!" I shout and pound the backstage door with both fists.

Calamity Crossing—good name for tonight. It's going to be a long, wet walk home.

Chapter Twenty-One

"Luka is a bookie!"

"Huh?" I wake up with Alex looming over me. What's going on? It feels like I haven't slept. My head is pounding. "What did you say?"

He jabs me with a finger. "What time did you get home last night?"

When did I get in? I rub my face. "I don't know—one thirty? I didn't have bus fare."

"So what, you walked? All that way? What happened to your buddy Luka?"

"I—he stayed. What's wrong with you?"

"What's wrong? We have a big game. Remember? And a bus to catch."

Right! What time is it? I fling back the covers and feel around on the floor for my jeans. Come on—where's my cell? I fumble in the pockets.

And blink. It's only 8:13.

I toss my phone. What the hell? The bus doesn't leave until nine! Why is Alex so ticked?

Back up, back up—oh no. I hold my head in my hands.

"I asked Dad about Luka last night. Know what he said?"

Here it comes.

"The only Luka I know is a bookie."

"I can explain—"

But he's not even listening. "And then Gil said, *That makes sense. The car, the phone, all the presents.* He said that he hopes you're not gambling." He stares down at me. "You're not, are you?"

Wait—Gil? All of a sudden, I'm on my feet. "What was Gil doing there? Is that why you were so happy I had plans? You wanted to go to the game with him?"

I shoulder past. I don't need the answers.

He trails behind me, too stunned to speak. But that won't last. And I definitely don't want to be there when it wears off.

I turn around to face him. "You know what? Don't bother waiting for me. I've got nothing to say to you anyway."

I slam the bathroom door in his face.

Ten minutes later I'm on my way. I half expect to see Alex waiting. But he's probably halfway across the park by now.

Good! I didn't want to talk to him anyway!

I charge into the park, kicking every stone I see.

I can't believe Alex gave my seat to G.I. Joe. Or that he told Dad about Luka. Did he tell Dad we hang out? Or did he just ask who Luka is?

Dad never listens to us. Maybe he didn't pick up on it. Luka wasn't there to ask.

Yeah, he was busy dumping me for a stupid card game. Some friend. It took me over an hour to walk home.

I kick another stone, and it nearly hits a runner. She gives me a dirty look, and I scowl right back.

I start chewing on what Gil told Alex. The gifts and the phone and the car *make sense*? What does that mean? Did Dad hear him say that? Did Alex tell Mom?

Halfway across the park, the wind picks up. It starts to drizzle, then rain. Soon my shirt is soaked, and my shoes squish. I swear at the dirty gray sky as loud as I can.

Then I run.

Chapter Twenty-Two

The bus pulls into the Lancers Center the same time I do. I hop on before the team even leaves the building.

I sit by my soggy self. I want to keep it that way too. Alex walks right by without saying a word. G.I. Joe's right behind him, studying me like I'm a math problem.

Danny plops in the seat beside me. Figures.

"You and Alex fighting?"

I look back at my brother and Gil. "Not fighting, exactly. Avoiding each other. Besides, he's sitting with Soldier Boy."

Danny makes a face. "That's taking one for the team. Maybe Alex can talk him into passing."

"I'd rather he talked him into enlisting."

He laughs. "I like it. Or leaving."

If I could just talk Danny into leaving, I might catch up on the sleep I missed.

I lean back and close my eyes.

But he doesn't take the hint. "So?"

When I don't answer, he elbows me in the ribs.

"I'm trying to sleep!"

"No way. Not until you tell me how it was."

I sigh. "How what was?"

His eyes bug out. "Are you serious? Calamity Crossing!"

"Oh. Yeah."

"Did you meet them?"

Did I ever. If you can call it that. "Yeah."

"And...?" He leans forward.

I put my hands over my face and breathe out. "Danny, I'm tired, I'm wet, and I'm grouchy. I will tell you all about it later. I promise. I'll even give you the T-shirt they signed."

His eyes get wide. "Seriously?"

"Sure. You can look at the pictures I took too." I unlock my phone and throw it in his lap. I tilt my seat back and close my eyes. "Just let me sleep."

"Deal!"

I wake up to a million cell phones ringing, all over the bus. "What's going on?"

I'm not the only one asking. Everyone's saying, "Hey!" or "What?" or pulling out a phone.

Danny stands in the aisle, holding my phone like a microphone. "Good morning, passengers. We're now landing in Greenwood. Please turn off your electronic devices..."

"Danny!" says Julio.

"Figures," someone behind me mutters.

Danny starts laughing. "You should've seen your faces. Looking around—*hee-hee!*—feeling

for your phones! I should've videotaped—
oof!" Someone throws a pair of socks at him.

"How'd you do that?" Alex asks.

"PhoneList. On Jack's iPhone. You can
set it to dial a list of numbers all at once.
It's for conference calls. Or wake-up calls."
He fiddles with my phone, and the phones
all ring again. "See?

"And I have to say, guys, those are some
seriously lame ringtones. Except for yours,
Jack. Calamity Crossing is awesome."

Danny grins at me until he sees my face.
I grab my phone back and stuff it in my
pocket.

*Calamity Crossing is lamer than you
think.*

And at game time, so are we. It's like
we forgot everything we learned overnight.
No one's where I need them. Except Gil,
who is always wide open.

No way I'm passing to him. He can beg
for the ball all he wants. I'll give it away
before I give it him.

My head hurts and my shoes feel glued
to the turf. It's my own fault, which makes

me twice as angry. My cranky mood rubs off on everyone. We're chirping at each other. We're chirping at Gil. And we're losing by two goals.

So Gil goes after the ball even harder. He picks up a bunch of fouls. Then, just before half, he takes out a guy's legs, studs up. The ref gives him a yellow and a warning. But it could've been a red.

Danny walks off the field with me at halftime. "He belongs in Port Peterson," I mutter.

Danny says, "Let's get him a written invitation."

Coach hears us. He pulls Alex aside. "You're the captain," he growls. "See if you can talk sense into them." And he walks away.

One look at Alex, and I want Coach back. I've never seen my brother this mad. Ever.

He grabs a fistful of my shirt and drags me over to Gil. He takes Gil's shirt in his other fist. "See these uniforms?" He gives us a shake. "When they're the same color, you're on the same fricking team!

123

"That goes for you too," he says, looking right at Danny. "It goes for all of you!"

He lets go of our shirts and points to the Greenwood bench. "Look at them over there. They love how we're playing. They don't have to beat us. We're beating ourselves."

I tug my shirt straight with a scowl. "Then give your buddy man of the match. He nearly got ejected."

"Yeah," says Danny. "If that was a red, we would've played short the rest of the game."

Gil blows up. "How else am I supposed to get the ball? You want more goals?" he fires back. "Send me the fricking ball. Or could St. Jonesy score without it?"

I take a step closer to him. "Let me tell you something, Soldier Boy. Jonesy didn't just score goals—he set them up."

"You're screwing me over because I don't pass like Jonesy?"

"No!" I throw my arms up in the air. "Because you don't pass at all. Ever heard of give-and-go, pass backs, overlaps? Or don't they teach that in those fancy European academies?"

He clamps his mouth shut and kills me with his eyes.

"Team?" I spit the words out one by one: "You don't even know what that means."

"I sure didn't learn it from you! You don't play me the ball—you don't even talk to me. None of you!"

He tosses my own words back at me before storming off. "Team? *You* don't even know what that means."

Alex shakes his head at me. Then he goes after Gil.

Before anyone can speak, I say, "Fine. Soldier Boy wants us to pass? Let's give him just what he asks for. Every time he calls for the ball, give it to him."

Julio frowns. "Every time?"

"Every fricking time. We've already lost anyway."

Alex drags Gil back. We take the field like we're all muttering "I'll show you" under our breath.

We make Gil work for every ball. He dodges head-high bullets. Races for slow rolling passes. Chases it to the sideline like a dog after a tennis ball.

He makes a run for the net, with two men on his tail. He's looking for a through ball, but I drop it behind him instead. Somehow he sprints back, turns the ball and lets it go. And boom—it's in.

Danny sends him a waist-height rocket that could've had him singing soprano for a week. He directs it in with his hip. We're back in the game!

Greenwood starts to mark him harder. Even that works for us. Gil starts using his options.

I feel like dropping to my knees and singing hallelujah.

He sets up Julio for two and back-heels it to me for a third.

We win it 8–3. And for the first time, we play eleven to eleven.

Gil walks off the field with me. "So that's how Jonesy played. Who knew?" He gives a bitter laugh.

My face burns. "Jonesy would never do that. He was a great guy." I blow out a breath. "That was us. Me. Being jerks."

"I know all about jerks. I played in enough cutthroat academies." He looks away, and his jaw gets tight. "No point in getting attached. If you're not the right piece for their puzzle, that's it—you're gone. And I'm just a shooter. It's not like I have the game sense you and Jonesy have."

But everyone's got game sense. Then it hits me. Not chess-move-early game sense, like me.

Gil can't see the game. None of them can. I feel special and awful, all at once.

"Gil, we would've lost today if it wasn't for you."

It takes him a second to answer. I can't read his face when he does. "Make you a deal. You keep feeding me the ball, and I'll keep shooting. And passing too. Okay?"

We shake on it.

"By the way, nice goal at the end," he says. "Just like Rooney."

I blink. "Thanks."

Alex spots our handshake. He calls a cease-fire with a nod and half a fist bump. Neither of us says it out loud, but it means no more questions about Luka and no more sniping at Gil.

Maybe this whole thing will blow over. Without blowing up.

Chapter Twenty-Three

It all comes together against Port Peterson.
We use the skills Coach taught us and the
tricks that we honed on each other to cut
down our opponents. We're unstoppable.
Determined. United.

It's how we could've played all season.
Crisp passing. Pretty touches. Strong cuts
to open space. Three options for every
pass. As unpredictable as a pinball game.
Everything we practiced, using every player.

Julio scores off a corner five minutes in.

I steal the ball back and angle a pass upfield. Danny sends it down their throats.

Gil catches a long ball on the volley and *bam!* It's in.

I jet into space to score the last goal. Roll the ball past the keeper and just inside the far post.

Port Peterson never gives up. It takes every man and three yellow cards to fight them off. But when the final whistle goes, the score is 4-0.

We're going to the semis.

The celebration on the field doesn't stop on the bus. If anything, it's louder.

"We Are the Champions" blares at the back.

The chirping and the chatter. The thump of someone hitting the floor. The laughter. This is how it's supposed to be. This is a team.

Alex comes to sit with me.

"Too loud back there for you?" I ask.

"Too rowdy. I got tackled less by Port Peterson."

Alex leans back with his hands behind his head. "You know, a month ago I wouldn't have said it. But the way we played the last two games, we might just pull this off."

"We're a million times better." I pause for a moment, considering. "We're even better than when Jonesy was playing with us."

"Never thought I'd hear you say that."

"Me neither." Feels disloyal, but it's true. We've all improved. Even Gil.

Chapter Twenty-Four

Today is June 30. That spells payday! I haven't looked at my account all month—it's been taking care of itself. But only one of my bets didn't come through for me. I'm going to get a decent wad of cash.

It'll be the first time I've seen Luka since the concert. We've texted back and forth a couple of times, but it's been busy.

I may as well figure out what the July games look like. I pull out my phone and log in to my account.

Wait—what? That's not my balance. I don't owe—$2,923! But that's my name...

I text Luka and he texts right back.

be right there

"Luka, something's wrong with my account. I don't know—maybe I was hacked." I'm sitting in his car, staring at my phone.

"Let me see." He takes the phone from me and tilts it so he can see the screen. "Looks right to me, Jack Attack."

"It's not though! I should be up $455. But it says I owe"—my voice gets tight—"almost $3,000." I point to the extra charges that start May 1. "Look! There's a whole new column!"

He doesn't even glance at it. "The interest."

Interest? And then I remember. *Ten percent. Daily. You don't want to get behind. It adds up. Very fast.*

Oh no. I grab the phone and swipe the screen. Scroll back through.

I sag into the seat. He's right.

Those bets I made to cover my losses. They weren't big enough. My balance has been growing all month. And now...

Now I owe Luka $2,923. And the amount goes up 10 percent a day.

"But I can't—where will I find—" My voice comes out like a siren. "I don't have that kind of cash!"

"I know." His mouth twists into a lazy half smile. "Don't worry, Jack Attack. I told you. We can work something out. Some people would gamble on any game, you know. Even yours." Luka watches me closely. "And with a little help from you..."

I lean away from him. "I don't—I don't understand." But I think I do.

I have to get out of this car. Right now. I fumble for the door handle.

"Think about it, Jack Attack. I'll be in touch."

I sit on my bed, twitching. I need to fix this—fast. But how? How will I ever get that kind of cash? Would Danny buy my phone? Might get me a few hundred. Would someone lend me the money?

No, whispers a little voice. All you need is one big win.

One more bet. I grind my knuckles into my temples. That's how I got here.

I scroll through the upcoming games. The Montreal game Thursday—$3,500 should do it. I do the math for three days of interest and groan. Better make that $3,600.

What if I lose? What then?

Chapter Twenty-Five

I'm falling. My parachute won't open! The ground rushes up in a dizzy blur.

I squeeze my eyes shut before I crash and...

Wake up on the floor, tangled in my sheets. Another bad dream. The last one, if I'm lucky.

The sun's not up yet, but the birds are. I tiptoe out of the house to run off the dollar signs. Running slow and easy just lets everything roll around in my head. Better turn on the juice.

The juice. I'll never catch up.

My heart pounds like I'm playing the biggest game of my life. My stomach is still in free fall.

When I win the bet tonight, I won't owe Luka anything. I could close the account. I'd never have to bet again.

If I did, I'd be more careful.

But if I lose tonight...

If I lose.

I won't.

I can't.

Because if I do, I owe $8,000. To a bookie.

I spend the day at the Lancers Center, trying to turn off my brain. But no matter how hard I concentrate, no matter how hard I work, my eyes drift to the clock. I give up trying and head home.

Alex is on the couch. "Game's about to start. Are you watching it, Jack?"

The pregame show is on. It flashes the lineups. The hosts make their predictions. How will it end?

"Jack?" Alex waits on my answer. "You watching?"

Am I?

"Jack, is everything all right?"

I squirm inside. For a minute, I feel like spilling the whole dirty mess. But what can he do? I roll my shoulders and take a deep breath. By the end of the game, it'll all be over. One way or the other.

"Jack?"

I shake my head and go to my room.

I'm afraid to watch. But I'm more afraid not to. I follow it on my phone, hunched over the screen. I grip the phone so tightly that my hands ache.

Everything hangs on the next ninety minutes.

I hold my breath and make a wish. Win it. Win it. I'll never bet again if you score right now.

The minutes crawl on. My phone gets slippery with sweat.

Then Alex cheers.

Refresh. Refresh. Refresh. Offside—no goal.

And then it's all over.

The phone rings in my hands seconds later. I check the display—Luka. I switch it to *silent* and shove it under my pillow.

But I pull it right back out. What's the balance?

I fall back on my bed and put my phone on my chest. It feels like someone has parked a car on me.

Can I really owe $8,180? I throw the phone against the wall and start gulping for air.

I can't fix this. Not now. Not ever.

There's no way out.

Chapter Twenty-Six

The next day, my stomach is still in knots.

The semifinal is two days away, and we're hosting it. Coach pushes us extra hard our last practice. The pressure's on. Everyone from the players to management wants us to win it at home.

I restock the treatment-room cabinets and help out in the boot room. Coach is always asking for help with the young teams. I fill the gaps with extra workouts and game films. The harder I work, the less I think.

Alex finds me on the elliptical around six.

"Heading out soon?"

I shake my head. "Tell Mom I'll be home late."

As late as possible. Partly because I can't face another night of staring at the ceiling. Partly because I'm avoiding Luka. At least until I figure out how to pay him.

Luka's not avoiding me. His car prowls through the parking lot. He's been calling and texting all day.

He texts again when I'm leaving the training center.

pay up, jack attack

I hesitate, then turn off the phone. I'll call him tomorrow.

I jog through the darkness, following watery circles of light across the park.

Going around a bend, I almost run into someone. I skid to a stop.

"Sorry, I—"

"Jack Attack."

His voice knifes through me. I want to bolt, but my feet won't listen.

141

The gravel crunches under his feet as he steps closer.

"Where have you been?"

I flinch and back away. Right into two big guys.

Luka's eyes gleam in the dim light. "I text. I call. What, we're not friends anymore?"

I hear the truth. We never were.

"I—I tried to—"

He snaps his fingers. His friends hoist me by my arms and drag me off the path. Can't—fight free. I've watched enough police shows to know what comes next. My heart bangs in my chest.

"Let me g—unh!"

Pain flashes, red on black. Can't breathe. I dangle by my arms, limp and gasping.

Another sucker punch. Another bright burst of pain.

And another. Need—air!

Have to get—away. I try to wrench free and groan.

"Luka, I'll pay—" Cold metal against my head. A gun? I shudder and jerk away.

"Yes. You will."

Click.

"Please. Don't!" I squeeze my eyes shut. Long seconds pass.

"There's another way." He brings his face close to mine. "A way no one ends up dead."

I gulp. "Not dead...is good. How?"

"You work for me." His words brush my face. "Starting Saturday at your semifinal."

"I'll be on the field."

"Exactly. I tell you the spread. You make it happen."

"You mean...cheat?"

"Control the score."

"If I do this—"

"When." He pats my cheek, hard. "*When* you do this."

"Wh—when. That's it, right? We're square?"

They let me go, and I pitch forward onto the grass. Their footsteps fade into the night. But Luka's voice is clear and cold. "I will call you with the spread."

I stagger to a park bench, hugging myself so my insides don't fall out. I'm shivering like it's the middle of winter. When I think my legs will carry me home, I brush myself off and start walking.

Mom meets me at the door.

"Good news! I got the weekend off. And your dad's free too. We'll be there to see you play!"

"See me what?"

"Play. The semifinal."

I squirm. Or see me *not* play.

She frowns a little and looks closer. She feels my forehead. "You're pale, and your skin is clammy. Everything okay?"

I hesitate. Should I tell her?

Sure. I can hear it now. *Hey, Mom. Can I borrow eight grand? I blew it gambling. Oh, and my bookie wants to kill me.*

I laugh, and it comes out broken. I press a hand against my abs.

"You're not okay." She puts her arm around me and shepherds me to the kitchen. "Is your stomach bothering you?"

My voice is shaky. "Just sore from practice."

"Sit down here and let me look at you."

Stupid Mom-radar. "No, Mom. I'm fine. Would you just leave me alone?"

It comes out sharper than I wanted. She jerks her hand back.

"Sorry, Mom. I'm okay. I just need a good night's sleep." I trudge upstairs to bed.

Chapter Twenty-Seven

Luka calls on the morning of the game. I'm afraid to answer. But I'm more afraid to ignore it.

"Jack Attack. Lancers are favored to win by two. Our bets are on Vancouver."

"You want us to lose? I can't do that!"

"Listen. Two-point spread. You lose, we win. You tie, we win. You win by a goal, we win. But if Lancers win by more than one goal, you lose.

"You *lose,*" Luka repeats. "Understand?"

And he's gone.

How can I do this? Screw up too much, and Coach will pull me. Play too well, and we'll score too many goals.

"What's the matter?" asks Alex. "Aren't you excited?"

I put on a big smile. But my teeth are clenched so tight my jaw aches. "Sure. Best day ever! Just a lot to think about."

"I know! I mean, we should trample all over these guys, but still..." He bounces up and down on his toes and stretches his fingers. I wish he'd just shut up.

The door opens and Gil comes in. Never thought I'd be glad to see him. But now Alex talks to him instead.

Win by a goal. No more than a goal.

Before long, everyone's here.

I feel like heaving. Sweat crawls down my back.

Alex elbows me. "You okay? You look a little green."

I nod.

"I don't feel so great myself. And just look at Gil."

A muscle's twitching in his cheek.

"Don't sweat it, Jack. Just pour it into the game."

I nod again.

A goal. No more than a goal.

Alex punches me in the shoulder and heads to the net. I give him the thumbs-up and nod. Gil stands on the left, buzz cut bleached by the lights.

Here we go.

The ball comes straight for me, right from the kickoff. Vancouver fans out, moving in fast-forward. The ball zigzags between them. Short, neat passes. I check for support and charge forward to slow my man down. Balance on my toes, wait for it. Watch his hips.

"On him!"

But I'm too slow. He dekes by me like I'm a pylon.

I sprint after him, but he's gone. Someone else picks him up. He gets a shot off, but Alex tips it wide.

They're good. Really good.

Goal kick. The ball sails up the field. Danny traps it and sends Gil in on a through ball. Julio races up the line. Gil finds him, then heads for the back post. It comes in laser-fast, and Gil side-foots it into the corner.

Goal! We're 1-0 and two minutes in!

Before I know it, they're on us again.

The play surges back and forth, back and forth. I'm caught in the ebb and flow. Struggling to keep up with a faster pace, a stronger offense. I rub my shoulder—a rougher game. No wonder Vancouver made it to the semis!

And then I remember.

That one moment is all it takes for my man to sneak by.

I'm on his tail, but I'm not fast enough. He chips it. Alex leaps up, and his fingertips brush the ball. But it's not enough to send it over the bar.

Alex kicks the ground and scoops the ball out of the net. Tie game.

I never thought that keeping the spread down would mean letting Alex down too.

Heather M. O'Connor

I don't know if I can do this.

We pull ahead by a goal in the second half. Then we pull ahead by two. So when a Vancouver player dances in, I hesitate. Just for a split second.

Maybe it's the stress. Lack of sleep. I don't think I let him turn me on purpose.

I chase him hard all the way to the net. That's how I see it happen. Just like in the movies. Everything slows down. I see it clear as can be. But I can't move fast enough to stop it.

Shooter's going full tilt.

Alex sprints right at him.

Shooter fires at the last second, flat and low and rock-hard. *Boom!*

Alex dives for it. Snags it. Hugs the ball.

Shooter can't stop. He leaps over Alex. And as he goes over, he clips him in the head with his cleat.

It takes forever to reach him.

"Alex! You okay?"

My fault—it's my fault.

That's all I can think.

Betting Game

He sits up and rubs his head. He blinks a few times when he sees us all crowding around.

Coach kneels down beside him. "You all right, lad?"

"Yeah. But it feels like a truck hit me. Did I make the save?"

"You did." Coach grins. "And the nice policeman there is giving the truck driver a speeding ticket." He points to the ref holding up a red card.

The trainer is pretty sure Alex doesn't have a concussion, but Coach sends him off anyway. A few minutes later, I join him when I roll my ankle on a late tackle. We watch the last fifteen minutes from the sidelines.

It's the hardest fifteen minutes of my life. Because I'm cheering for the Lancers to win. But I'm afraid Vancouver won't score. And if they don't score, the biggest loser will be me.

When the final whistle blows, our team goes crazy. Alex and the rest of our bench run onto the field to join them. But the team won't abandon me. Gil and Danny run over and hoist me on their shoulders. They carry me into the celebration.

I don't know whether to laugh or cry. Not because of my ankle. Because the final score is 3–1.

I lose.

The celebrating ends. The locker room clears. Reality hits.

Win by a goal. That's all we had to do to make everyone happy. But we won by two. I pound my fists against my head. How much did Luka put on the game? He's here. I know he's here. What will he do when he finds me? My stomach lurches. I probably deserve it for what happened to Alex.

I can hardly catch my breath. I think I'm going to puke. Then I hear these ugly sounds. They're coming from me. I'm crying, and I can't stop. All of a sudden, I'm a leaky balloon.

Alex sits on the bench beside me and waits for me to pull it together. He bumps his shoulder against mine. "What's going on, Jack?"

I search his face and look at the lump on his head. "You're okay, right?"

"Sure, I'm okay." His forehead is all scrunched up. "But you're not."

"I was afraid—I'm so sorry!" I see it all again. I slam my fists into my head, but I can't make it go away. "That was my man. I should've stopped him. I could've stopped him."

"You tried."

"I did. I swear I didn't do it on purpose. H-he wanted me to lose, but I was trying to win. You believe me, don't you?" But if I can't convince myself, how am I going to convince Alex?

"Believe you? Believe what? *Who* wanted you to lose?"

Just then the door to the showers crashes open and hits the wall. A dozen empty water bottles wobble on their shelf and tumble to the floor.

It's Gil. He blows past us, slamming locker doors and kicking over the garbage can.

153

Then he wheels around and comes back. Before I know it, he's grabbed my jersey and hauled me to my feet. His hands are shaking, like he's holding a grenade and he's already pulled the pin. Any second he's going to blow.

Alex doesn't say a word. He just stands up so we're shoulder to shoulder. Gil's eyes flick from Alex to me. We're frozen like that. Then he lets me go and wipes his hand off, like he's handled something filthy.

"Told you it made sense, Alex," he growls. Then he kicks open the door and storms out.

It doesn't take Alex long to put together the pieces. His eyes open wide, and the tips of his ears get all red.

"Gil was right! About Luka. About everything. You've been gambling."

I sit down with a thump. "Since April. On the first team." I look up to meet his eyes. I swallow hard. "I lost a few bets. Not a lot. But it adds up."

"So you owe him money." Now it's Alex who looks like he smells something rotten. "How much?"

I mumble, but he hears the number clear enough.

His mouth drops open. "Ten grand? How can you lose ten grand in three months?"

I give a bitter laugh. "Yeah, I can't believe it either."

"I still don't get it." Alex puts his hands on his head. He paces away and back. "What does that have to do with our game?"

"Luka said—he made me promise—to—"

"To what? Lose? You tried to make us lose?"

"No! Not lose. Just...not win by as much." I can't look at him. I bury my head in my hands.

"You let me get kicked in the head for a bet?" He cranks up the volume. "You risked the championship? Gambled with the future of every guy on that team? For a fricking bet?"

"Look, I know, okay?" I stand up, and now it's me yelling. "I know! But what was I supposed to do? He put a gun to my head. He told me what to do. Or else he'd—well, or else. He's probably waiting outside to jump me right now."

"A gun?" He sits, hard. The bench shudders under his weight. He looks at me. "A real gun?"

I remember how cold the gun felt. "Pretty real."

Alex's breath goes out in a huff. "What have you gotten us into?"

He looks at the door, then back at me. It's like we're seven years old again, figuring out how to tell our parents we busted the kitchen window with the soccer ball. Again. He's just as lost for answers today.

He sighs. "We'll work something out. Okay, bro?"

Protecting me from Luka? Covering a gambling debt big enough to buy a car? We aren't seven years old anymore.

"You think he was at the game?" Alex asks.

I nod.

"Then he saw what happened. It wasn't your fault, right? You tried."

I just stare at him.

He blinks. "Okay. So, he's pissed. As long as we can get to Mom and Dad, we can get to the car. He can't cover all the exits. And he has to get us alone."

Us. Somehow, knowing Alex is on my team makes me feel a little better. Then I squirm. I bet Alex doesn't feel any better.

Chapter Twenty-Eight

"How are we going to get out of here? He could be waiting anywhere."

"I guess we—*shh!*" Alex puts a finger to his lips.

Steps. Coming down the hall.

No time to hide. Nothing to defend ourselves with.

We close ranks, with our backs to the wall and our eyes on the door.

I hold my breath. My heart's banging like I just finished suicide sprints.

Go past. Just keep walking.

The footsteps stop right outside the door. I look at Alex and make like I'm ready to run. He nods.

The door swings open.

We jump a mile high.

It's just the security guard. He stares at us and chuckles.

"Didn't mean to startle you." He looks around and checks the showers. "Anyone else here?"

We shake our heads.

"I'm locking up. I'll walk you out. Your folks are waiting down the hall."

He'll walk us out! We relax a notch.

"Congratulations. I hear you fellas won."

He keeps up a steady stream of conversation while we pack our stuff. I feel like a bobblehead doll—my head just keeps nodding and nodding.

"You go on while I get the lights." He walks into the showers, and his voice is muffled. Light switches go *click, click, click*.

I reach for the door handle but can't bring myself to touch it.

The guard is back. "Out we go."

He holds the door open, then turns out the lights. We look both ways, cringing at the hollow *clang* and the scrape of the key in the lock and the guard's voice echoing through the halls. He doesn't seem to notice.

We turn the corner, and I see Mom and Dad waiting for us. Thank goodness.

And then I see who they're talking to. Blond hair. Mirrored shades. Luka.

Mom sees us first, and her arms open wide. "The heroes of the day! What an exciting game. I'm so proud of you."

She hugs me first, then holds me out at arm's length. "How's the ankle? Does it hurt much?"

I duck my head. "No, it's okay. Or, at least, it will be. It's all taped up."

Alex is next. "I was so worried when you went down." She tips his head to look at his eyes. "Your pupils look okay. No dizziness?" she asks, feeling his goose egg.

"Ow! Mom, it's just a bump on the head!"

Dad hugs us next, pounding on our backs a little too hard. "Way to go. Best game I've seen all season. Worth the price of admission! Isn't that right, Luka?"

Luka shakes Alex's hand. "Good game."

Then he grips mine, and I feel the small bones crunch together. "Way to win it, Jack. I thought you were going to lose, but you pulled off a win, didn't you?"

He says all the right things, but I get his message loud and clear. When he releases my hand, I flex my fingers.

"See you around, Jack."

Don't bet on it.

As we're leaving the stadium, Dad takes Alex and me by the arm. "This calls for a celebration. What'll it be, boys? Burgers? Pizza? Ice cream? Whatever you want, it's on me."

Just the thought makes me feel sick to my stomach. What I really want is sleep and a locked door. And a plane ticket to Peru.

"Can I get a rain check, Dad? It's been a long night."

"You sure?"

"Rick, they just played a hard game," Mom says. "They have another big game tomorrow. They need their sleep. Let's go home."

"Yeah," says Alex. "We don't want any trouble with Coach."

We have enough trouble already.

A black Stingray peels out of the parking lot, and I watch the red taillights until they're gone.

Mom takes another look at me. "You all right?" She hugs me again, and I'm afraid I'll tell the whole ugly story.

"I'm fine," I tell her shoulder and myself. "I'm fine."

Chapter Twenty-Nine

Alex and I lie in our beds talking. I tell him about meeting Luka, and how cool it was to talk about soccer with him. How exciting it was to watch a game that I bet on.

"He listened to me, you know? He asked so many good questions. About my system and the Lancers and sports medicine. But I guess he was just bleeding information. He was just setting me up." I search Alex's face. How can I make him understand? "I felt so smart. So cool. So...respected."

"You never figured it out?"

"Not really."

But if I'm dead honest? I close my eyes. The phone, the questions. The car. Concert tickets to a band he doesn't listen to.

I blow out a breath. "I don't know. I guess I didn't want to figure it out."

"Dad never asked you about it?"

I shake my head.

He frowns. "And you don't want to tell Mom."

"I didn't even want to tell you."

"Why? I'm your brother. We've always—" He looks at his hands, and his voice gets quiet. "But not so much lately."

"No. But that's not why." I've been blaming everyone else so long that the words stick in my throat. Once I start, they pour out. "Look. I met Luka before Gil even got here. What happened...it was my own stupid fault.

"If it means anything, I wish I had talked to you. Maybe I wouldn't be in this situation. Captain America always saves the day."

"Captain America?" It makes him laugh.

"Sure. He's not the coolest superhero, but he always does the right thing."

"Thanks. I think."

He stares into space for a few minutes, tapping his fingers on his bed. Then the tapping stops.

"I know how you can get the money."

"How?"

"Our scholarship account. It has about $15,000 in it, right? Mom will probably find out eventually, but..."

"...but if I got a job, maybe I could put it back before she does!"

Perfect! I could be out of this mess by—

"Wait. Half of that money is yours."

"You just said you'd put it back, right? So problem solved. Now go to sleep."

And I think maybe I finally can.

My phone wakes me up before the alarm goes off.

It wakes up Alex too. "Hang on," he whispers. He gets out of bed and sits beside me. "Put it on speaker."

"Hello?"

"Jack Attack."

"Luka. I tried, but—"

Alex elbows me and mouths, "Tell him about the money."

"B-but I have what I owe you now. All of it."

"What you owe us?" He laughs. "What about what you cost us?"

"But—"

"Here's what it will cost you. A broken knee, a fractured skull. Yours or your brother's. A terrible car accident. It happens. All the time. Maybe your Mama can pay. We'll collect on her way home some night. It's extra, like juice. Understand?"

The phone feels cold in my hand. What have I done?

"I will give you one more chance to pay. The game today. Who would your system tell you to bet on? The Lancers. Of course. Everyone says it. So. Make a liar out of your system." His voice gets hard and cold. "Lose this game. Don't win. Don't tie. Lose. Or you will lose, Jack Attack. Something far more precious than a trophy."

I stare at the phone. There's no way out. And now—Alex. Mom.

Alex takes a shaky breath and lets it out slowly. "I guess we need a plan B."

Chapter Thirty

When we get to the locker room, there's no plan B. But Gil's there.

Alex and I exchange looks. Did he tell Coach? I close my eyes and brace myself.

"I heard what you said. After the game."

Alex says, "Gil, I—"

"I want to help."

"Help? Help *me*?" That's the last thing I expected.

He chooses his words carefully. "Team is

about passing the ball around, right? Using support when someone offers it?"

"Yeah." I blink. I guess it is.

"Then what's the plan?"

And the weight pressing on my chest eases up.

Alex lays out the situation. How much I owe. The interest. The threats.

It's even more humiliating when someone else tells it.

Gil's eyes widen a couple of times, but he listens in silence.

Alex winds up. "And so we worked out a way to pay him—"

Gil breaks in. "Back up. The bookie—he says you're working for him?"

I nod.

"It won't work."

Alex and I exchange looks.

"It's not money he's after. It's control."

Alex looks confused. "Why would he turn down $10,000?"

"That's pocket change. These guys bet more than that on one game."

Baby bets. Nickels and dimes. That's what he called it.

"He's right." They look at me. "The day I met Luka, he threw down $1,000 because of something I said."

"On a tip from a stranger?" Alex says. "No way!"

But I wasn't a stranger.

"He knew who I was. My name, my team, my position." It fits. I press my head between my hands. "He knew all along."

"It happens in Europe all the time." Gil sighs and rubs his chin. "They go after the guys who control the game. Wine and dine them, give them expensive gifts. Once they get their hooks in..."

He looks at me and shakes his head. "Jack, they'll never let you go."

Never. How could I be so stupid? I tip back my head and put my hands over my face.

Alex says, "Then..."

"He'll get threats. Or worse."

I raise a hand. "Already happening."

"If he's caught, his soccer career is over."

Over?

"So what can we do?" asks Alex.

But before Gil can answer, Kim, the physio, bustles in. "Coach was right, Jack. He said you'd be here already. He wants me to take a look at that ankle before the game. Maybe tape it."

"It's fine. Really!" I hold it out and swivel it. "See?"

"Heard that a million times." She laughs. "You know the drill. It won't take long."

"But I need to get ready."

"You're not going to miss the game. Honestly!" She hustles me out.

I look over my shoulder at Alex and Gil. Alex flashes a thumbs-up. Gil just gives me a worried smile.

I hop onto the treatment table. Kim pulls up a rolling stool and turns my foot right and left, forward and back. "Normal range of motion. A little swelling. Bit of bruising." She looks up. "No pain?"

I shake my head.

"Looks good then. But it won't hurt to tape it." She tucks my foot between her knees and gets started.

My phone bings. A text from Luka.

choose what u lose—game or family

It chimes again. It's like driving by a car accident. I have to look.

This time it's Alex.

tell Luka to come to the locker room after the game for his $$$

I text back.

this is plan b???

He answers right away.

don't worry

just play hard

Kim taps my foot. "You're done. How's it feel?"

"I guess we'll see." I flex my foot. "Thanks. Wish me luck."

"You bet!"

I hop down from the table and text Luka.

have ur money. can we talk after the game?

His answer makes my hands shake so bad, I almost drop the phone.

screw with me and ur dead

Alex and Gil better know what they're doing.

The locker room is buzzing when I get back. There's nowhere to talk to Alex or Gil. No time either.

My uniform is folded on the shelf above my locker. Before I grab it, I rub my nameplate for luck.

Coach comes in as I'm tying my cleats. Everyone quiets down. We wait for Coach's usual patter and last-minute instructions. But today he doesn't say a word.

He takes a good long look at each one of us in our Lancers uniforms. He clears his throat. All he says is, "You lads know why you're here. Make me proud."

Alex and Gil and I look at each other and give a little nod.

"Let's do it!" I say.

And we're on our feet chanting, "Championship! ChampionSHIP! CHAMPIONSHIP!"

Chapter Thirty-One

I take my position on the field, bouncing on my toes. Jump up a few times. Loose. Limber. My breath comes out in nervous puffs.

The game. Focus on the game. Teamwork.

Win. We have to win. I close my eyes. But win or lose, I lose.

I take a couple of deep breaths to calm my nerves.

If I have to lose, I'll do it with my head high.

I check over my shoulder. Alex is nervous too. He sidesteps right, tags the post. Sidesteps left and does the same. He leaps up to touch the crossbar. Adjusts his gloves.

Then he looks at me and shows me a clenched fist. *Let's do this.*

I hold up my fist in answer. And all around me, our teammates do the same.

Port Peterson wants revenge after the 4-0 smackdown. They're dishing out the blood and bruises to prove it.

They keep hitting us hard, hitting us late and hitting us dirty. Tugging our jerseys. Throwing an elbow or a fist.

We just concentrate on playing our game. They can't keep up with our first-to play and one-touch passes.

Especially my buddy number 10. He barely gets the ball. When he does, I steal it back and laugh. The more I laugh, the madder he gets. And the worse he plays.

He tries to avoid me and rams into our defense. They intercept him, box him in. No one's fooled by his fancy footwork.

It makes him crazy.

I laugh to myself. *We know just how to shut you down.* We practised all season on Gil.

Gil uses his size as well as his skill to take the hard hits for the offense. No matter how hard they try to trip him up or push him off the ball, he gives it right back.

Twenty minutes in, he barrels through their defense and sets up Julio for a pretty little tap-in. Julio times his run perfectly, but he's mugged at the edge of the six. He gets up limping but shakes it off.

Five minutes later, Gil finds him again and runs in for a cross. But the cross never comes. Their defender takes out Julio's legs in a late tackle, and Coach and the trainer have to carry him off.

We all get mad, but Gil gets even. The referee awards a penalty shot. Gil places the ball on the penalty spot. Their keeper tries to read which way he'll shoot. But he's wasting his time. Gil scores before he can move. No windup, just a bullet into the corner.

I pump my fist.

But there's no guarantee we can hold a 1-0 lead. Especially after two of our defenders get injured, one after the other, just before halftime. We've used up all three substitutions, and our bench looks like a hospital ward.

We need to keep scoring. We also need to stop number 10.

Chapter Thirty-Two

I'm so caught up in the game, I forget about Luka. At halftime, my phone flashes a reminder. I grab it and head for the bathroom.

Luka has sent me a selfie of him, Mom and Dad all giving a big thumbs-up from the stands. Real subtle.

call me

I dial his number. It only rings once. He starts talking right away.

"So nice sitting here with your parents. We talked about so many things. Your mama, Janis. Such a fine woman."

I hold my breath.

He keeps going. Each slow word digs deeper. And suddenly I have no breath to hold.

"Pity she works such long hours. She comes home so late. Nice house. Good neighborhood. But crime happens everywhere. Even on Carling Road. Must be what—six blocks from the bus stop to your door?"

"Shut up!"

"Or your brother..."

"Shut up!"

"The game is not going well. Don't disappoint me, Jack Attack."

Chapter Thirty-Three

Port Peterson is starting to wear us down in the back.

The new defenders struggle with the rough stuff. Whenever they back off, number 10 sneaks in for a dangerous shot on net. Alex has stopped every one. So far.

One shot could turn the tide of the game. We need to shut down number 10, and we need to score again. So how do I play it? I'm torn.

Danny goes down at the seventy-five-minute mark, his nose gushing blood.

The trainer takes a look. "Pretty sure it's broken." He holds a pad against Danny's nose to soak up the blood.

"I can play, Coach," says Danny in a muffled voice.

"No, lad. You can't."

"But we don't have any more subs!" he protests as they lead him to the bench. "Don't take me out, Coach. We can't play a man short for fifteen minutes!"

That decides it. "Don't worry, Danny!" I shout. "I got this." I drop back to shore up our defense.

They keep pounding us. We keep holding them off. But we're not getting any chances ourselves.

And we're slowing down. I'm slowing down.

The ball goes out for a corner, and I line up with Alex. "Can't be much longer."

"Couple minutes," he says.

They're desperate to tie it up. The corner sails in, and Alex leaps up to pick it out of the air. While he's airborne and unprotected, number 10 elbows him in the head.

Alex hits the ground, and the ball jars loose. He scrambles for it on hands and knees. As he pulls it in, number 10 kicks it out of his hands and into the net. The whistle blows.

Tie game.

Gil shouts, "Aren't you going to call that, ref?"

Julio hustles him away.

Alex gets up, rubbing his head.

"You okay?"

"Yeah. Go!"

I grab the ball and go back to mid. We need that goal. Now. We'll never make it through thirty minutes of extra time. Not with ten men.

I bring the ball up the left. I'm just past half when number 10 comes at me, studs up. It should've been his second yellow, but it's just a free kick.

Gil trots back. He leans in and whispers, "You and me. Teamwork. Let's show 'em all."

I nod. "Deal."

And that's how we score the prettiest goal of the game.

I set up the free kick just inside the touchline, making sure the ball sits just right. Gil lines up with the defenders, about thirty yards out.

"Time, ref?"

He shakes his head.

One chance. We've got one chance.

I send a long hard ball into the eighteen-yard box.

Come on, Gil.

He times his run perfectly. He fakes out his defender and races for the box.

The keeper sprints off his line. They're all closing in.

The ball's coming down, but he's not quite there.

Come on, Gil. Hit the gas.

He launches himself headfirst at the ball. G.I. Joe to the rescue!

He head-chips it over the keeper, then belly flops onto the turf. The ball sails in, just like van Persie's Flying Dutchman goal!

Then it's over. We did it! We won!

Gil's on his feet already, buzzing around in circles with his arms out like a fighter jet. I run after him, laughing and shouting, "That was brilliant! The craziest thing I ever saw!"

He grins at me and pumps his fist in the air. The team mobs us. Guys are doing chest bumps, backflips and the best collection of bad dance moves since disco died.

I glance at the stands. Mom and Dad are making their way to the field.

Luka hasn't moved. I feel him glaring at me through his mirrored shades. When he's sure I'm looking, he aims a finger gun. *Bam, bam.*

I start to shiver. Alex notices first, then Gil.

I give them a shaky smile. "Tell me you have a kick-ass plan B."

The celebration carries on around us. Pictures and hugs and applause. Handshakes from the league and the club. Speeches. Alex accepts the big golden trophy and waves us all in to hold it up. Laughter when it nearly falls on our heads. And each time I look, Luka's still sitting there on his phone.

Watching.

Waiting.

Chapter Thirty-Four

The celebration is finally over. We've relived every epic goal. Every heroic save. Every awesome tackle and pass. There's nothing left but dirty socks, sweaty uniforms and the three of us.

And one terrifying text.

big mistake

Now we kick off a more dangerous game. Alex and Gil have explained the plan. Everything is set up.

"Text him," says Alex.

"Okay." I give them a crooked smile and a thumbs-up. "Here goes plan B."

I pull out my iPhone and close my fist around it. It takes me a couple of deep breaths to unclench my fingers and turn it on. When I do, it just sits there, slick and shiny. Harmless.

This better work. My phone may be bulletproof. But I'm not.

i can explain. i have your money

where r u

the locker room

alone?

yeah

I put down my phone and stand in the middle of the room. Alex and Gil circle around with last-minute instructions.

"Keep him talking."

"But stay cool."

"Yeah. Don't make him mad."

"Stand right there. Don't move."

I swallow. "Got it."

"And don't forget—"

"Got it. Just go."

The door closes with a bang, and it's so quiet, I can hear my breath.

Footsteps. All at once the door opens. Luka comes in. But he's not alone. He's got two big buddies with him.

We're already off the playbook.

Luka walks right up to me. He shoves me back a step. "Are you stupid?" Shove. "You couldn't lose?" Shove.

He's keeping his voice down. Good. Not good.

"You were down to ten men. For fifteen minutes!" He backhands me, and I stumble back. "And you couldn't lose?"

I hold one hand up to my face. Calm. Stay calm. But my heart is banging.

"No. You had to win. Just like yesterday. Big mistake." He raises his hand again.

"I told you! I–I can pay you." I back away, holding up my hands. "I have the money!"

"Too late for that."

Stay cool. Don't make him mad. Keep him talking.

"But I can still help you. With my system."

He looks back at his buddies. "I love gamblers with systems. They make me rich." Their laughter bounces off the walls.

My face gets hot. "Then why did–?"

"You were useful." He rolls his eyes. "Talk, talk, talk. Who is in. Who is out. Who is coming back."

"I didn't mean to. I thought you–"

Just stand there. Breathe in, breathe out. Keep him talking.

"I know. Our little career talks." He's right in my face. "Have you seen the car I drive? You think I need a university education?"

His voice drops to a guard-dog growl. "You're the one that needs an education."

Don't. Run. Don't. Fight back.

He shoves me again and again. "I'll teach you–what happens–when you don't–listen–TO ME!"

He snaps his fingers. One of his thugs rams me into my locker. My head bounces off the shelf so hard I see stars.

Water bottles rain down and roll around on the floor. And my phone falls too.

It tumbles off the shelf behind me and bounces off my shoulder. It clatters onto the tile floor in front of me, dragging my eyes with it.

The screen doesn't break. The phone doesn't even stop recording.

Luka scoops it up. His eyes flick from me to the flashing red light.

Danger, danger!

The corner of his mouth turns up. He turns the phone so it videotapes me.

"Say goodbye, Jack Attack."

Chapter Thirty-Five

All at once, Calamity Crossing blares from my phone. Luka nearly drops it.

Then his phone rings.

A rap tune plays across the room.

"We Are the Champions" comes from the showers. And a whole chorus of sirens from the hall.

Luka freezes.

"Jack! Come on!"

I dash for the showers. The door slips open, and Gil and Alex pull me inside.

We force the door shut. Lock it. Lean on it.

Just in time.

They pound on the door. What would those fists have done to me?

Then we hear a crash. It's the locker-room door.

"POLICE!"

I breathe again. I slide down the door until I'm sitting on the cold tiles. I start shaking like someone dumped a cooler of ice over me.

Alex and Gil give each other high fives. They whoop and jump in the air. The sound rebounds off the walls and rattles around inside my skull.

Alex crouches down. "You okay, Jack?"

I nod and lean my head back. "Ow! Except for this lump on the back of my head." I touch it and wince.

I was terrified of Luka. But what comes next is pretty scary too.

The police march off Luka and his muscle-bots. It gets very quiet in the locker room.

"You can come out now," says a voice from behind the door.

Alex and Gil strut out. Easy for them. They're heroes. I lag behind.

A police officer looks us over. "You boys okay?" she asks.

We nod.

"Which one's Jack?"

I take one slow step forward.

"We have a couple of people who want to speak to you."

That's it. I'm going to jail. I hope she doesn't take me away in handcuffs.

She opens the door. Mom and Dad rush in. Coach is right behind them.

And for once, I can't find the words.

Chapter Thirty-Six

Two hours and a trip to the police station later, Dad drives Mom and me home. Coach, Alex and Gil are already there, sitting around the kitchen table. They stop talking the moment we come in.

"So?" asks Alex.

I take a deep breath. "I won't be charged."

The tension lifts. Questions bubble up.

"What happened to Luka?" Gil asks.

"They arrested him. He'll probably get off with a fine. I'm not on the hook for the money. But I will have to testify."

"Just a fine? Won't he come after you?" asks Alex.

"That's what I was worried about," says Mom. "But the police said he'll back right off."

"The gambling ring is based in the Ukraine," Dad explains. "Jack's account is small potatoes. They'll write it off as the cost of doing business."

"Especially Luka," I add. "The fine's a slap on the wrist, but coming after me could land him serious jail time. He'll just go fishing for another gullible player."

"The officer told me I'm lucky I followed my teammates' good advice. I did the right thing. Eventually." I mimic the detective's frown and serious voice. "*Using rather unconventional methods. Not something I recommend.* But she also said it was creative. And effective."

Heather M. O'Connor

"I heard her tell the story twice while we were there," Dad says. "Using PhoneList got big laughs. Especially getting the police to set their ringtones to sirens."

"Nice touch, Alex," says Gil.

They slap their palms together.

"You were right, Gil. What they really wanted was to get their hooks into me." I swallow hard. "They would never have let me go."

I fight the burning in my throat. "I just want to say I'm sorry. To all of you. Thanks for sticking by me."

"And for rescuing you," says Alex.

"Creatively," adds Gil.

I give a shaky laugh.

Then I turn to Coach and force myself to look him in the eye. "I don't know what to say, Coach. It was a really stupid mistake."

"It was," he says sternly. He pats me on the shoulder. "But it won't happen again."

My chest gets tight. "That's for sure. They'll kick me out of the academy for this."

"Well, lad...that's up to the club. But I have a few ideas."

Chapter Thirty-Seven

Orientation Day. Cars pack the Lancers Center parking lot. Parents and players are milling around inside and out like tourists at Disneyland. Guides are already leading around groups. The new players are easy to pick out—the wide-eyed wonder is a dead giveaway.

I walk past the trophy case. It's lit up brighter than a night game. I double back to admire the new addition, a golden cup big enough to hold a soccer ball. The inscription sparkles in the light. *National Champions—Durham Lancers Academy U17-U18.*

Gil walks up as I'm standing there. "Looks good."

I grin at him. "So good I want to keep it for another season."

We bump fists and join the rest of the team in the dining room.

"Seen our trophy yet?" I ask them.

"Yeah. Seen our schedule?" asks Danny. "First game's in two weeks. Guess who we play."

His face gives it away.

I groan. "Not Port Peterson?"

"Ding-ding-ding! That is correct."

"I hate those guys."

We talk about summer and school and the new season until Alex says, "We're up in five minutes. Ready for Coach's speech?"

"As long as we get to hear Jack do it first," says Danny.

"Yeah!" the other guys chime in.

"Okay, okay." I stand and muss up my hair. I hold the back of a chair like it's a lectern. "Awrrright, lads. I have a few rrrules."

I stare at Danny. "I want your eyes and ears on me at all times. So no cell phones on the field. No texting. No exceptions."

I wag my finger. "Now, practice is at 5:00 AM, twelve days a week. You must be on time, every time." I tap my watch. "Or you hand-wash all the socks and knickers."

That gets a laugh from everyone.

"Those of you who think you're the next Messi?" I scowl at them, one at a time. "You're sadly mistaken." I point to Alex and Gil. "You needn't look further than these two lads."

Alex grins and shakes a fist at me.

"Ha!" says Danny. "Some things never change."

But one thing will. I'm making a speech of my own this year, for a team of my own. I'm coaching the Under-10s as part of my community service.

I bet some smart-mouthed kid will imitate me too. But I wouldn't put money on it.

Author's Note

The match fixing in *Betting Game* was inspired by real events in the CSL, a Canadian semiprofessional league. Though two academy teams played in the CSL at the time, they were not involved.

Match fixing is a global problem. Slick criminals like Luka do target soccer players. That's why teams as young as Under-12 are beginning to attend sessions on match-fixing prevention and education.

The academy teams in the story are completely fictional, with a ten-month season and schedule loosely based on the U.S. Soccer Development Academy.

Acknowledgments

This book was a team effort.

My critique group, Critical Ms, kicked it off. Thank you to Erin Thomas, who showed me the way; Bill Swan, who showed me the news; and Ruth Walker, Gwynn Scheltema, Kim Moynahan, Jocelyne Stone and Nora Landry, who encouraged me through thick and thin. I'm also grateful to my extended writing family: Writescape, the Writers' Community of Durham Region and CANSCAIP.

To my dear pen sisters, Theresa Dekker, Deb Rankine and Ruth (again), thanks for writing yourselves into my life.

My thanks to the team at Orca Books, especially my editor, Amy Collins, for your patient coaching and generous feedback.

Thank you to John Lay for the learn-to-play clinics that put me on the pitch, and to my teammates on the Durham Divas, especially Jill Stewart, for making the beautiful game so much fun. I'm also grateful to my home club, Whitby Iroquois, where at least one O'Connor has played, refereed or coached every year since 1991.

Thanks to the experts who supplied important facts and details—any mistakes are mine. Toronto FC gave me a peek into academy life and a tour of the KIA Training Ground. Detective Sergeant Bill Sword told me what makes Luka tick and explained illegal gambling and game fixing to a writer who won't bet a quarter on a card game. Elite players Tyler Swan and Jordan Sutherland graciously answered many nosy questions.

Most of all, I thank my home team—my husband and kids—for the boundless support. You hugged me when I was grouchy, listened patiently when I read and advised me on soccer and teenagers and cell phones and bookies. Special thanks to my daughter Anne: you helped me kick the soccer and the plot into shape. I love you all. You make my life a beautiful game.

Heather M. O'Connor knows all about warming up a keeper. Three of her kids played keep for rep teams. In 2006, after fifteen years on the sidelines, the devoted soccer mom bought some cleats and joined a team. Heather is a freelance writer, editor, author and mother of five (and grandmother of two). She lives in Whitby, Ontario, with her family and her yellow Lab, Lady. Her biggest thrill while writing this book was touring the Toronto FC Training Ground. Go, Reds!

orca sports

For more information on all the books
in the Orca Sports series, please visit
www.orcabook.com.